PIXEL

THE HUNGARIAN LIST

THE HUNGARIAN LIST

Series Editor
Ottilie Mulzet

ALSO AVAILABLE

László Krasznahorkai
Destruction and Sorrow beneath the Heavens
Translated by Ottilie Mulzet

Gábor Schein
'*The Book of Mordechai*' *and* '*Lazarus*'
Translated by Adam Z. Levy and Ottilie Mulzet

PIXEL

KRISZTINA TÓTH

Translated by Owen Good

LONDON NEW YORK CALCUTTA

HUNGARIAN BOOKS
AND TRANSLATIONS
OFFICE

PETŐFI LITERARY MUSEUM

This publication has been supported by a grant from
the Hungarian Books and Translation Office
at Petőfi Literary Museum, Budapest, Hungary

Seagull Books, 2019

ISBN 978 0 8574 2 609 3

British Library Cataloguing-in-Publication Data
A catalogue record for this book is available from the British Library.

Typeset by Seagull Books, Calcutta, India
Printed and bound by WordsWorth India, New Delhi, India

Contents

The Hand's Story

The hand's fingers are short and chubby, and the nails are chewed to the quick. The hand belongs to a six-year-old boy. The hand's fingers help with counting and covering the eyes. The boy sits on a stool scribbling circles in tailor's chalk on the tabletop, despite being asked not to a few times already. He draws the lines spiralling outwards, imagining that if he goes on drawing circles for ever without stopping, the lines will gather on top of one another and rise from the table up into the space, like a spring. He had tried to explain this to the others but no one would listen, so now he's working alone, his head tilted to one side, covering the drawing with his arm. He found the chalk in a drawer where the grown-ups had hidden it. The little boy is called Dawid, by the way, he lives in the Warsaw Ghetto with his mother, Bozena, and her sisters. Someone kicks in the door, the three people in the room press into the corner. When

Celina jumps to her feet, she notices the chalk, but she can't say anything about it now, because she's been shot. The chalk drops to the floor and breaks in two. Later, when some strangers are searching through the drawers for cutlery and linens, someone steps on it. Unfortunately, Dawid isn't able to finish the chalk experiment, because he doesn't survive the war. He dies in Treblinka.

Sorry, wait. He doesn't die in Treblinka. And he's not even a boy, but a little girl. But then all these children are so alike: nails all chewed to the quick and pudgy, stubby fingers. The hand belongs to a little girl, and the girl's name is Irena. She's Lithuanian and from Vilna. Wait, I'm talking nonsense, I'm trying to tell you everything at once. How could she be Lithuanian! She only looked blond at first glance. She did, she looked blond but her hair is actually rather dark and curly. In fact— and this is the truth—her name is Gavriela. She was born in Thessaloniki, and arrives at Auschwitz in February 1943. She survives the war but loses her mother and her home. Later, she'll settle in Paris and become a French accountant. Yes, it can happen.

Her husband is a very nice, thin-haired official at BNP Paris, but this has nothing to do with our story. Gavriela thinks in French, forgetting her Greek. More and more often she hears her mother's name, Domna, as if the French for 'curse' were echoing within it. She speaks only French with her children and reads Greek literature in French translation. Her hands are truly ugly, her fingers are short, that's why she doesn't wear jewellery given to her by her husband. She keeps it in a leather case. Gavriela isn't happy, because even in Paris very few can manage that, but, to be honest, she's content. She has a girlfriend with whom she goes shopping.

This friend looks remarkably like her: when they sit beside each other on the metro, the passengers take them for sisters. Incidentally, the friend is half-Romanian, half-Hungarian, and also has greying curly hair. I know, it seems more confusing by the second, but there's no way to smooth out the straying, tangled strands of reality into a shiny tassel. The friend's hands are just as ugly but she doesn't worry about that any more—she's old.

A long time ago someone walked away from this hand, abandoning it. Her mother had a lover back then in Cluj-Napoca. When the news went around that the ghetto was going to be cleared, this lover got hold of two safe-conduct passes. The mother agonized for three days, then left with her lover and abandoned her then four-year-old Cosmina. She'd rather save her own life, she thought. She put a parcel in the girl's arms and left, she didn't even look back. This happened in the Iris district, on 13 May 1944. The only reason all this is interesting is because later Cosmina's son was born on 13 May, and he got the name David. Naturally, this has nothing to do with the other boy seen in the Warsaw Ghetto, who had the same name but whom everyone later forgot. This David wasn't forgotten. His Hungarian great-grandfather, who somehow survived the hell of war but not Ceaușescu's Kingdom of Heaven, lived just long enough to hear of his great-grandson's birth. And he thought the name David was a bad idea, but that's another story. The boy, though, didn't learn this story of abandonment from his great-grandfather (and a good thing too) but from the other residents of the brick-factory ghetto who, at the time, angry and horrified, had nursed the orphaned Cosmina.

That's a lie, but somehow it seemed right that way. David never even knew that someone had abandoned his mother's hand. In any case, there was nobody left who could have met him, and who could have explained to him how Cosmina's mother pleaded with her lover to give her both the passes, and how, in her enamoured and confused head, eventually the desire to live won. Gavriela doesn't know this story either, she heard a different story about the hand left abandoned. She heard that all of this happened in far-off Lithuania, in Vilnius, and that the little girl was actually called Irena. That Irena's hand had been abandoned and Irena's mother was the one who'd left her daughter. And Gavriela also imagined that neither of them survived the war.

None of this is certain of course. The names revolve around us, it would be difficult to follow up on each one. Most often we have to rely on assumptions. The chalk experiment, for example, is feasible in theory, after all, the lines have extension. Presumably, Dawid was correct. If one were to draw circles for an endless length of time on the same surface, then after a while, the line of the drawing would rise off the table in a cone shape and create a tangible bulge different from the knots in the wood. You could test it on paper, but to this day nobody has ever had the patience to do it for long enough.

The Neck's Story

'Mum, don't be stupid, you are not old!' The woman was standing in the corridor in front of the fitting rooms trying to shove her mother back in. The Germans waiting with dresses over their arms watched them uncomprehending, while the older woman of the two just shook her head, she seemed unyielding. The problem wasn't that she had caught a glimpse of herself from behind in the double mirror—that she had seen the wide bra cutting into her back, and her tatty, grey hair. This could have been what the problem was, but it wasn't. It didn't even bother her that her daughter was going to pay for the dresses—her daughter was earning well and her German husband even bought his mother-in-law the odd trinket. This was a completely different story. The older woman had come across something in the fitting room and couldn't tell anyone about it. Her face was burning but she couldn't say why. She could never tell her daughter the neck's story.

In '78 she went to the West for the first time in her life. Not that she went so often later on, but that first trip had been particularly memorable. She'd been invited to a conference in Ulm. The girls were still small and her husband was watching them. It wasn't customary for the doctors to bring X-ray assistants along, especially not for a five-day conference in the West. She assumed the senior consultant had arranged the trip, and she also assumed that he wanted something from her.

When they pressed up against each other in the corridor one night, she knew she'd end up following him into his room. Both of them had been drinking and it was hitting her pretty hard. Heads spinning, they fell onto the bed and made love until dawn when, at about five o'clock, the doctor sobered up and quietly slipped off, as though he had been called to attend to a patient.

She didn't get up until half past eight. In the bathroom she noticed that he had given her a hickey on her neck. Nothing like this had ever happened to her, and she began to worry that it wouldn't disappear within three days. She had her breakfast in the hotel, then set off into town with her travel allowance. She ended up in the women's section of a department store. The sex-filled night and the free morning ahead of her were liberating, and she didn't feel the customary, sudden pang of guilt that overcame her anytime she set about shopping for herself.

She stepped into the fitting room with a red low-cut dress. She would never have picked such a showy dress for herself at home, but here she figured she could pull it off. She saw herself in the mirror and a woman's sky-blue eyes stared back, the type of woman who could easily wear red for a few more years.

She turned to have a look from the side, and that's when she saw the scarf on the hook. Someone must have forgotten it. The silk neck scarf was red and blue with some sort of logo on it. She had never stolen a thing in her life, nor did she intend to steal this, she simply wanted to try it on. It suited her and it covered the mark on her neck perfectly. She took it off and put it back on the hook, so that if the owner came back looking for it, she'd find it. She was just about to leave the fitting room when her heart started thumping wildly and an eddying desire came across her to go ahead and take it. A silk neck scarf for a red dress. She looked up at the ceiling, as though she were afraid someone might be watching, and then stuffed the scarf into her bag. At the checkout she felt like the cashier could see through her, like at any second she'd point to her handbag and have her take it out. Or some customer would pounce on her and interrogate her about what happened to the scarf they had left in the fitting room. But nobody even looked at her when she paid and no one followed her when she left the store with the shopping bag in her hand. On the escalator, on her way down, the beating of her heart finally subsided.

That afternoon she wore the red dress and the scarf to the conference, where she gave a slide show, their presentation. The scarf brought out her bright blue eyes. The senior consultant then gave a longer speech in German that she didn't understand, but she felt as though throughout it everyone was staring at her breasts, and that despite her two children people still found them enticing.

That evening she left the scarf on for dinner, and later she allowed the doctor to knock on the door and repeat the previous night.

Now, twenty-nine years later, as she was trying on dresses, she suddenly lost confidence, and the usual anxiety came over her—what's the point, anyway. She peeled off the uncomfortably tight blouse and went across to her daughter's fitting room. She tugged back the curtain and stepped inside. Her daughter was in the process of trying on a sweater, and she called out from inside the sweater, Is that you, Mum? Her head popped out at the top, but instead of her dyed-blond hair there appeared a piece of bright fabric. At first her mother thought she had got tangled up in her slip. Then she saw that she was wearing a kerchief on her head that covered her face like some sort of veil. She pulled the silk kerchief from her face and hung it back up on the hook next to two others, exactly the same. 'They put these everywhere,' she explained, 'or at least in the nicer places. It's so the customers don't muck up the clothes with their make-up when they're trying them on.'

Without a word the old woman turned and left the fitting room. She recalled how, back in '78, she had stood there on the podium wearing that department store's kerchief and she was certain now that everyone had seen where it was from. There was that red-and-blue stripe across it, the same as on the company's shopping bags. And now she was convinced they had spotted the purple mark beneath the kerchief, the stolen love, and her husband left at home with the two little girls. Like how in an X-ray she could see things the patient would never guess.

'I don't need anything,' she said to her daughter wearily, and beat a path through the people waiting in line, like she'd do in the hospital corridors with a diagnosis in her hand, hoping not to be accosted by the next of kin.

The Eye's Story

The woman is sitting in the Budapest metro right beside the door on the end of the row. Exactly where Gavriela and Cosmina were sitting in a metro car from a different story. And myself, your narrator—or rather the voice you can hear, sometimes fading, sometimes perfectly clear, like during the radio broadcast of a theatre show—I'm sitting directly opposite her in the stuffy car of the present day. I hadn't noticed her until now because I was standing, but a seat opened up across from her. At times like this you can't help staring at people, unless it's so crowded that the pressing clothes block the view.

The woman's clearly blind. Sat firmly upright with dark sunglasses. All kinds of bags by her side and the thin white stick beside them. Its little plastic nose for tapping the way is resting on the floor beside her shoes. Wow! She's in high heels. A vain, slender, blind woman. I'm sure she's sitting beside the door because when she got on, somebody offered her their seat.

The next stop comes and several people stand up, blocking the passengers opposite from view. Meanwhile I think about the blind, I have their cautious and gentle walk in front of me, always prepared for a sudden stop. That distinctly raised head. How they never look at their feet.

A lot of people get off. The space frees up again in front of me and I can see the row of seats opposite. She's still there, perched stiffly in the seat. She could be around fifty-five or sixty, but she's the kind whose age you can never guess. She's wearing an elegant brown skirt and a similar coloured jacket. Her nails are painted. On her finger there's a strikingly large and intriguing ring. It's angular with a sandblasted surface, and a heavy thing by the look of it. There's no knowing if it's a wedding ring or not, but perhaps it's too wide. Not your everyday piece of jewellery.

We're approaching the next stop and someone stands in front of me again. I think about the varnished, light-pink nails. It's difficult to paint nails, even for sighted people, it takes practice. The woman must not paint them herself. She gets them manicured, which means she wasn't always blind. It's a habit left over from her old life that she won't give up. Or rather she lost her sight. She must have a sad, ageing husband who always compliments her nails. Or there's a manicure girl in the city who knows everything about her, the woman would even take her sunglasses off in front of her. She sets down her sunglasses on the little table while she soaks her nails in the little dish. No. She has a daughter, tortured with guilt, who regularly paints her nails, and they spend quite some time discussing the colour beforehand. The daughter hates her mother's veiny hands, and the acetone smell makes her stomach turn.

I can see her again, and I look at her face now and her hair. She's taken good care to have it trimmed and dyed, she must visit the hairdresser at least twice a week. No doubt this is for her sad husband too. She used to have gorgeous blue eyes but she lost her sight in an accident. A car accident. No. A tropical eye disease. Her husband is a diplomat and they were living in some exotic country when she was infected by an incurable eye disease. She was even treated in Switzerland, but they were only able to find a temporary cure, though they spent an enormous amount of money on the operations. No. She had gorgeous amber eyes once, that's what her husband really fell for. Then a few years ago, the optic-nerve tumour was diagnosed and she lost her sight. She doesn't consider herself blind, she's just adapted to this unusual and frankly outrageous situation. No. She has green eyes and she's only blind temporarily, like love. She's had a retina operation and for a few weeks she has to be careful of bright light, hence the sunglasses. She got the white stick at her husband's insistence, because it was prescribed, but she's ashamed of it. When she collected it, she kept picturing the familiar shop window with the mastectomy swimsuits and almost turned back. When she actually made it into the neighbourhood medical-supply shop her heart was pounding. In the end passers-by will think she wears a prosthetic or something. She was still worried that maybe someone had seen her from the tram. Should have gone to a different shop, she thought, but she'd already known this one because she'd been coming home this way for years.

A crowd pours in and the people getting on block her from view. Something's bothering me but I can't quite put my finger on it. Like a detective I start piecing together the details in my head and I can tell there's an anomaly, something doesn't add up. Suddenly it pops into my brain and I see what's wrong. I'm delighted with myself, like an inspector who's just realized there's one tiny detail in the story that doesn't fit the whole picture.

That's it! That's what's wrong! She's wearing a watch! Why would she wear a watch? She could just be wearing it as jewellery. Another habit left over from her old life that she's relentlessly clinging on to. The gold watch is hard to put on—she has to fiddle with the clasp. Her husband usually fastens it for her and gets frustrated because it's so difficult. But he doesn't dare ask what the point in keeping it is. He's been too scared to ask anything for years, he'd only ever answer, but even then with caution. And any morning he's late he blames that bloody watch, or his wife, because yet again he was the one who had to fiddle with the clasp.

The crowd drifts towards the door. I spot her high heels among the shoes. Apparently she's stood up. She's moving for the door and I can see her now from head to toe. She's got paper bags in one hand with a home furnishing store's blue logo across them. But the white stick isn't tapping the ground in the other hand. No, the white stick is a curtain rod with a plastic tip. The woman isn't blind.

The watch she's wearing isn't from a son, she does have two sons, but this watch is from her daughter Helga, that's right! It's a fake. It doesn't even keep time, because on the platform the woman sees the metro clock is twelve minutes ahead of her own. The watch cost five euros and the daughter got it at the seaside in Greece with her man, saying, Whatever, that's what she's getting, it'll do. She didn't want to spend more because they had already bought a load of stuff and anyway she doesn't even love her mum.

The Leg's Story

The purple-haired teacher spins in the corridor. She can't see a women's room anywhere. She hates these offsite language classes, she barely found her way here, on top of that she didn't have time to pee before class. And her leg has been sore ever since the hot weather came.

There happens to be no one coming and she slips into the men's room. It'd seem this is all there is on this floor. She's just finishing and about to pull up her underwear when she hears the door swing open and somebody come in. He starts peeing in the urinal outside. Not to worry, he'll be gone in a second. She needs to be leaving soon for her next lesson if she wants to get across town before the Friday rush hour. It's a similar business class, at least three-quarters of an hour from here by car. She ponders which bridge to take. The man outside is still pottering about, not leaving and she's too embarrassed to come out. Two slow minutes pass, which in the text's time, for the reader, is hardly anything, but for the teacher it's nerve-rackingly long. It'd seem the man outside is taking his time on purpose. As though he was curious who's in there. But he couldn't have seen her shoes from outside, the toilet bowl was too far from the door for that. Eventually she can't bear it any longer and she comes out.

That very moment the man is positioning the crutch under his right arm—until now he had it propped up against the tiles so he could pull down his fly. The woman sees that he's in a cast up to his thigh. She wants to slip past but you can't exactly shove aside a man with his leg in a cast, so she awkwardly holds the spring-door open for him while he clomps past. He gives her a good look up and down meanwhile, and comes to the conclusion that middle-aged women shouldn't dye their hair purple.

He arrives in the lift at the ground floor of the office block, and only then does he think, Hey, that woman was pissing in the men's. But he doesn't have time to think on it because his taxi arrives to take him to the trauma ward. Today the cast's being removed. None too soon, he thinks, his stomach has turned completely blue from all the anti-coagulant injections. Plus last week it rained, he'd had to pull a plastic bag over the cast and he looked like a tramp.

While she inches along in the traffic jam, because of course she didn't manage to avoid the rush hour, his cast is sawn off with an amount of fuss and he's given a sheet of paper with the physio's number on it. He takes the crutch with him just to be sure, and as he crosses the zebra he leans on it slightly because his leg hurts from the sudden load. He feels liberated, his leg is unbelievably light, as though it wasn't even there. He doesn't check the road and a woman in a blue Suzuki suddenly honks at him, then points with sweeping gestures, Oi, it's red! The crutch only slows him down, he doesn't really need it, so at the next corner he leans it against a skip and calls another taxi from his mobile. The skip and pavement are heaped in rubbish because it's the neighbourhood clearing day, and the street is laden with the residents' useless junk.

An hour later the same street corner is thronged. Two paunchy men in track suits shuffle their feet as they lug a fridge. A broken corner bench and a torn recliner are added to the lumber, stained mattresses accumulate in a pile. There's a gypsy lady in a puffer jacket sitting on a cabinet with sliding doors, swinging her legs and nibbling sunflower seeds. The sinewy, forlorn-looking man who came with her tosses a crutch onto their heap of selected items, then goes about expertly taking a fridge apart. He takes care to coil up the cable, removes the cover, then cuts off the plug connector and puts it in his satchel. He is just about to start wrenching off the side panels when another group of metal collectors arrive on the scene. On the back of the truck are countless ironing boards, drying racks and other metal waste. The new group hop down and make to snatch up the fridge. Some pushing and shoving breaks out, then shouting and someone starts making threats in Romani. The woman takes a second from her sunflower seeds and calls over to her husband: 'Oi, leave it out! What do you want, eh? Get yourself taken to the Gulags?'

He shrugs his shoulders and steps aside, meanwhile one of the newly arrived lads spots the crutch. The nibbling woman throws over that it's for sale. The boy bends over and takes a good look at it. He tries it out, holding it under his arm and limping a few steps with it. A couple of people stand around him, reassuring him that it's just his size, he could make a few bob with it.

In the end he buys the crutch for two beers, but by the time he gets back from the corner shop the others have driven off. His older brother was with them on the back of the truck.

He grabs the crutch and limps to the crossing to practise a bit. It's a warm, smoky twilight, the air seems deadlocked and the line of cars isn't moving in either direction. The boy starts in the direction of the crossing. The support under his arm is really pressing into him now but he reckons he can get used to it.

The man liberated from the cast has arrived home. His calf and thigh are really throbbing. He vows that he'll never play football again, he shouldn't have pushed himself like that anyway. Last year he had a heart attack, he should be happy he's even alive. He thinks about his youngest daughter—he should give her a call. But then he'd have to start explaining what was going on and he'd feel ashamed. Meanwhile he draws the curtains because the low afternoon sun is shining in and he can see what a state the flat is. When he came in the door it was like an old man's flat, even the smell.

The purple-haired teacher flips down the sun visor and turns on the radio in the car. She's worried she'll be late. We can see the tailback from above, so we know she will—the blue Suzuki has no chance whatsoever of reaching her next lesson. Miles up the road at the bridge approach there's been a three-way accident, as a result, all of the lanes are at a standstill. A boy limps between the cars' running engines, and the teacher makes small circles above the pedal with her foot, she has a cramp in her calf. She does the kind of exercises you might do on a long flight. 'It's a pity the classes couldn't be further out of town,' she thinks. All of a sudden she spots a begging hand outside her open window. She quickly reaches for some change, and swears to herself that she'll go to the doctor. She grabs up more than usual from the change.

You can never be sure. She isn't superstitious, but she finds it odd that this afternoon, this is the third person she's met with a crutch.

The Head's Story

It all began during the Italy trip. His old tourist's reflexes were working and he did his best to see everything there was to see. A long time ago, the building engineer had worked in the preservation of historical monuments, and during this trip he made a point of looking at every single facade worth seeing in the little Italian city, and the palazzi along Via Garibaldi too. Meanwhile he swore he would never take on another lecture abroad, this was the last.

The next day, before noon, he was lying in the hotel room when the bed gave a lurch. It rocked back and forth, then slowly it began to rise and fall. The logical explanation would have been an earthquake. With tremendous effort he pushed himself onto his feet and staggered to the window to look outside. He saw a peaceful morning square, with some old bloke walking a dog and a blonde woman heading by in high heels. But as he lay back down on the bed the tremors hadn't stopped. His last conscious thought was to grab the little gold key from the dark-stained wardrobe opposite.

If he'd woken up later with the key in his hand, then he could have been sure the quake wasn't a dream. Yet when he came to, his hand was empty, but his clothes were drenched with sweat. His shoulders ached, because he had clung to the bed with every ounce of his strength a few hours ago, when the room had lost its solid outline.

After dark he strolled down to the ice-cream shop across the square. When he looked up at the cashier girl, wearing a white top and hooped earrings, he saw a large, amorphous blotch where her face should be. He suspected it was just sunstroke, but he swore that he would get himself checked out as soon as he got home nevertheless. Normally he would have to wait a month for the MRI, but he was bumped to the top of the list. They handed him a plastic pump and asked him to press it if he felt uncomfortable at any point during the scan.

Inside the thing it was like lying in some kind of coffin. The whole time he could hear this rhythmic knocking. As though someone were trying to dig him out from under the ruins of his life and, in the meantime, using Morse code to let him know they were getting close.

The ward's senior consultant presented him with the findings. She had remarkably big blue eyes. The remarkably blue pair of eyes rested in a sagging, mature face, but there was something appealing and radiantly feminine about the doctor.

At home the man distractedly watched the World Cup and decided not to say anything to his wife for the time being. What could he have said anyway? That recently he's been having strange hallucinations and a blue-eyed doctor has asked him to come in again next Tuesday?

That Tuesday they took a seat in the small office of the doctor. She noticed the ring on his finger, which he wasn't wearing last time during the MRI, because he'd had to take it off in the changing room. It certainly was an interesting thing. His wife had it made especially by a designer for their thirty-fifth wedding anniversary. It was round on the inside and angular on the outside with a sandblasted surface. He would never have worn anything like that himself, but given that he had long since stopped loving his wife, he wore it respectfully. The doctor chose to look at the ring rather than his face as she went through the diagnosis. She didn't tell him the truth, that is, she didn't say a single word about what the picture showed. She just mentioned he would need further scans and that certain signs might indicate a tumour. We have to explore every possibility, she said.

Had she told the truth, she would have first explained that the tumour was on the brainstem. She would have continued by telling him that soon he was going to lose his memory, and most probably his personality as well. That presumably he would become paralysed. She held the scans up to the light and pointed out which bits to look at. He thought they were like symmetrical inkblots and you could see all sorts of things in them. An owl, a Pekinese, a lion. True, she added, and a baboon, but he couldn't make out the monkey head. From time to time during the consultation she would look at his hand, trying to decide whether the ring was a wedding ring or not. She thought it was far too flashy, whatever it was.

The wife, on the other hand, was mad about unique pieces like that. While this very conversation was taking place she was strolling around an

IKEA and had picked out a large blue illuminated globe. Not for their own flat but for their daughter Helga's. Helga was thirty years old and had moved into the loft space of a newly built apartment building. The mother knew she couldn't count on any grandchildren in the near future, after all, Helga had been the lover of a married man for years now, but the mum had started furnishing the future baby's room anyway. She bought a white, plastic-tipped curtain rod and a few (in terms of our story) completely uninteresting bathmats.

Meanwhile, the brain tumour was also settling in, trying in its own way to make the occupied property, namely, the man's brain, homier. There were no thoughts about the wife spinning around his brain any more, in fact, let's admit it, with the new flat now, Helga and the two sons had all been driven out. At nine o'clock that night, with the MRIs in his lap, he phoned the doctor from the bathroom and told her he'd got the baboon.

The doctor never found out whether the clunky ring was a wedding ring or not, but she did accept the invitation to his country house near Villány. The little cottage had a porch and was built from sun-dried clay bricks, so it stayed cool inside despite the summer heat. He reeled off a well-practised speech about how he had salvaged the original ironwork and put in the wooden rafters, before tipping the blue-eyed doctor on the coarse, woollen throw.

The doctor's mature body wasn't remarkably beautiful, but he was still much happier to put his arms around hers than his wife's thin, forever cold-skinned body. As he undressed her bit by bit he noticed a deep and lengthy scar along her stomach. The doctor had given birth to both of her children by Caesarean and had told him a little about them on the road down, when they stopped at a small musty roadside tavern. During lunch she had told him how one of her daughters, Edit, had married a man in Germany and the other (Ági maybe?) lived on Baross Street in Budapest and had just turned thirty. She's pretty miserable, the poor thing, can't find herself a normal man. The engineer took out a photo of his three grown-up children and boasted to her that he had bought each of them a flat, but that he had put together this little house just for himself, and, actually, he'd just bought a nearby wine cellar to go with it.

The whole time they were making love the coarse, woollen bed cover itched horribly. She ran her fingers up his back and thought about how a good designer really has to think of everything, that's what design is all about. The angular anniversary ring irritated her throughout the fore-play but she thought it would be rude to ask him to take it off.

In the evening they sat out on the porch of the little house, and the doctor acknowledged quite contentedly that the man's phone hadn't rung all day because he'd turned it off. They sipped on the wine and stared into the falling darkness. Suddenly the man started squinting into the distance and pointed in surprise, saying hey, the water is rising, waves are coming in towards the porch, bigger and bigger ones, he doesn't understand. There aren't even any lakes around here. You're right, she said, look at how pretty the water is. How it reflects the moon. He could see perfectly well that there was no moon of any sort reflected in the swelling mass of water, plus he would have found the image much too romantic, but he didn't want to argue. On the one hand, he had a splitting headache—from the driving, obviously. On the other, he had fallen in love with this stranger, this blue-eyed doctor.

The Palm's Story

The mother set out the stuffed pepper and called through to the girl's room a second time that food's ready. But it was pointless. The girl didn't come, so she tapped on the door.

Her teenage daughter sat down at the table in silence. After two bites she put the spoon down. 'Don't you like it?' asked the woman. 'Well, if you want to know, it's pretty shit,' answered the girl and went back to her room, without even pushing in her chair. At first the woman wanted to scrape the leftovers into the toilet, but she thought better of it and tipped it back into the pan. A quarter of an hour had passed, so she knocked on the girl's door again. The girl was supposed to be at her father's by four o'clock but she hadn't even packed.

Since there was no answer she cautiously opened the door. Newspaper was spread all over the desk with open tubes of glass paint laid out on the paper. The girl was kneeling on a chair in stripy socks and degreasing the window.

'You want to paint now?!' asked her mum.

The girl got down from her chair and glanced up at her darkly: 'It's my window, isn't it? OK?'

The mother began packing her daughter's rucksack in silence and then closed the paints one after the other. She crumpled up the newspaper and brought it out to the kitchen. When she was done with the rucksack, she called through drily to the girl sulking on the bed: 'You've five minutes to get dressed. And air out that smell.'

The girl had been doing this for weeks. She simply couldn't stand the woman's boyfriend and tried to deprive her of opportunities to see him. Two Saturdays in a row she had stayed at home when her mother would have been meeting him. The girl had even been willing to sacrifice a school trip to the quaint town of Szentendre, just so that she could throw off plans at home. The last time, she'd threatened that if she saw that disgusting, hairy man next to her mother one more time she'd commit suicide. That was the first time the woman had ever slapped her daughter. Even she herself was slightly amazed to see her hand rise up and come down, as though it was her own mother moving inside her, controlling her muscles with seething rage. The girl clasped the red palm-mark on her cheek and stood there unable to speak as though she'd forgotten where she was, and who this upset and repulsive woman was in front of her.

That was two weeks ago. The woman had arranged to meet with the disgusting, hairy man again today, but the girl clearly didn't want to leave home. When she finally left, she jogged down the stairs without saying goodbye and slammed the door of the building so hard that the whole upstairs floor shook. The woman watched her from the bedroom window—she wanted to see whether she was going towards the trolley-bus stop. Later that afternoon, just to be sure, she called up her ex-husband, but the girl wouldn't come to the phone.

The weather had got cold, and gloomy low clouds descended over the neighbourhood. Neighbours hollered down to the children cycling outside, the dog-walkers went inside, and by around seven in the evening a heavy silence had fallen.

He was late, but in return he said he'd stay the night as well, which seldom happened. In fact—

let's be honest, at least in deference to the facts—
never. He was in the middle of a divorce with his
wife, but the unspoken agreement was that both
of them would sleep at home and they'd act as
though everything was perfectly all right. The
woman felt this was a pointless hypocrisy and they
discussed it a lot. At which point the last word
would always be the same: Well, you know best.
This irritated him no end, it sounded as though his
wife had cloned herself and was arguing with his
lover's tongue, too. He'd had enough of everybody
expecting something from him. For example, he
would have liked this woman not to want them to
move in together. He honestly couldn't stand her
daughter—he thought she was an aggressive,
specky little toad. (And she was.)

Really he wished for nothing else than to be
with her free of any obligations, all the time if possible. We could write—it'd be much shorter and
more elegant—that he loved this woman. But we'd
have to add that he did so in his own way, though
that wouldn't mean anything, after all, people can
only ever connect in their own way to another
being who, in their own way, expects and permits
this. In any case, the way this man had of doing it
would at times delight her and at others completely

baffle her. This very moment, for example, he was standing in front of the open wardrobe, and one by one he was burying his face in her dresses, taking in her fragrance, all the while repeating that he was positive he was experiencing his greatest-ever love. He loved expressing himself in such extremes. Holding the reheated stuffed pepper she curtly replied that it seemed she wasn't needed for that. And she went out to lay the table.

That night neither of them could sleep. They felt this was a rare gift of an opportunity but as though the endeavour and the self-consciousness were stronger than the actual desire: they were incapable of making love. Ashamed and covered up, they talked in the dark about the past. The woman said that as a child she'd had a dog and she'd like one now but she can't because her daughter is allergic to the fur. He'd never had one, he replied, but he'd gone out with a girl who had a big Alsatian. And then he told a story about his father who had been an alcoholic. They fell silent, eventually he turned on the bedside lamp and uncovered the blinking woman. He looked at her skin, the pale down which covered her body, her hair, her breasts spread across her chest which she quickly covered with her hands. He removed one of the hands, running his finger over the creases in her palm, and told her she'd live for ever. That's a bit much, she said, she'd settle for less, as long as he was with her. The rain outside pattered on the garages' corrugated roofs and they could hear the cars puttering by on the road. There was a huge clap of thunder and the windowpanes trembled. Then another, and the rain beat down harder and harder on the street. 'I'm cold,' she said, and sure enough she had goose bumps. 'The cold's getting in somewhere.'

The man got up, she could hear him close the tilt window in the daughter's room.

'It was open,' he said, and at last he made love to her, and left the bedside lamp on, although he knew it wasn't a habit of theirs, so he could see her face as they made love.

The girl didn't come home from her dad's until Sunday evening. She was excited because she'd been bought a new white jacket from Mango and a colourful scarf to go with it. She didn't ask about Saturday, she walked over to her mum and buried her face in her shoulder. Then she went into her room, she wanted to finish the mandala on the window which she'd started on Saturday.

Suddenly she dashed into the kitchen, fixed her gaze on her mother and hissed loathingly: 'Disgusting. You're both disgusting. You're pigs!

The woman didn't understand at all. She went after her into the bedroom. The teenage girl was sitting on the bed with her legs pulled up and pointing at the window, but there was nothing there. Or maybe there was. As she leant closer, she saw that in the middle of the window, where the girl had wanted to paint the mandala, quite clearly, was the print of a man's palm.

The Shoulder's Story

The Mickey Mouse on the sandy beach stands beside the girl in the swimsuit and hugs her. No, not beside the same girl—this is another story from another time.

The only similarity is that this girl isn't willing to smile either, she stares into the camera, plainly sulking. Mickey Mouse grabs her up and the child starts to bawl. Behind them the blue sea, in front of them the helpless parents. In the end they don't get a picture, the family heads off in the direction of the ice-cream shop. The Mickey Mouse lifts the head off and wipes his sweating brow, then peels the costume off down to his waist. A man in his thirties or forties, his back is soaking.

Gavriela and Cosmina watch him from their sun-loungers as he throws his head back to take a drink. The Turkish coast was Gavriela's idea, Cosmina had never been here before. The beach-goers think they're local Turkish women, but close as we are, it's clear they're speaking French. They have strong, curly hair and they aren't young any more, so both of them independently decided upon a black one-piece swimsuit. One of them is half-Romanian, half-Hungarian, the other is a Greek Jew, in other words standard French women with retired civil servants for husbands. They can't speak Romanian, Hungarian, Hebrew or Greek. Or any other languages for that matter, being French.

During the scene a moment ago, both of them thought of their sons. Gavriela asks Cosmina to put more sun cream on her shoulders. She has some already but the sun has moved and it's hitting her stronger. Cosmina stands up, blue veins run along her broad white thighs and her thick calves. She wipes the sandy cream from the bottle neck, does both of Gavriela's shoulders, then sits back down. They're silent.

Quite some time later Gavriela says thank you, then watches the water. The sea is hurling big waves at the shore, the shrieking bathers jump over the spray. She speaks suddenly, her son still on her mind.

'I wanted to tell you something.'

Since there's no response, she launches into it.

'You know, when Jean-Philippe wanted to die.'

'Yes.'

'It wasn't because of a woman.'

'No.'

Gavriela fell silent again, but perhaps she was just gathering strength.

'It was because of a man.'

Now it's Cosmina's turn, she's quiet. After a while she speaks, she speaks about David, her son. We have to add this because it isn't expressly clear from their conversation.

'I don't think I'll have grandchildren either.'

Another long silence follows, let's not wait for the end, how about we sum up what they say. The murmur is loud around them, and both women stop and start as they speak, so it isn't easy, but it's necessary. Cosmina expounds that David, her son, who is thirty-nine at the time of the story, wants to move to Romania for some reason. Yet he hasn't a single living relative left there. But first he'll spend a year in Hungary in a surgical department, then the next year he'll become a partner in a clinic. A beauty clinic to open next to Bucharest. He's already received the loans for it.

Gavriela knows perfectly well that David is already in Budapest, and she doesn't quite understand the whole story. That boy can't speak a word of Hungarian, what business has he there? There are clinics everywhere, why head off into the sticks. Not to mention hygiene. In truth, she isn't really interested because her thoughts are still spinning around her own son, Jean-Philippe. But she doesn't want to upset Cosmina and she answers.

'Why wouldn't he go? You can get married there too.'

By that she means to say, that at least he still has the chance of a family, not like her son. That he can bring some wife from the back and beyond too. In theory at least.

Cosmina doesn't know how to answer this, so she asks Gavriela to do her shoulders, because they're burning a lot. Gavriela smears in the cream while Cosmina drawls on.

'You shouldn't worry about that: that's who he is, end of. The point is that he finds his place. For some reason David can't find his. You know . . . '

Cosmina smears the last of the cream on her own shoulders and wipes a bit on her arms.

' . . . You know, it might sound stupid, but I think it's all because of the Jewish thing. That's the problem still.'

This topic usually bores Gavriela to death.

'But you're not Jewish.'

'Everyone's Jewish,' Cosmina concludes after a couple of minutes from behind her sunglasses.

Now this Gavriela doesn't understand at all, they sit in the sun. The Mickey Mouse man has found another child, this time they manage to take the photo with Summer Fun! written across the bottom.

At six o'clock in the evening the women finally stand up from the sun loungers, they shake the sand out of their towels. They slip into their flip-flops, and examine each other from behind. Both women's shoulders are scorched.

CHAPTER EIGHT, OR

The Ear's Story

The girl, christened Ági, rather than Ágnes, by her parents back when they still loved each other, didn't attach much hope to her thirtieth. She had just moved into her flat on Baross Street. Her birthday came after in November but in the end she spent it alone again, not even her dad called. It turned out later that on the day, he had been mourning the death of the great footballer Ferenc Puskás with real compassion, a candle burning in the window. Weeks later when the forgotten birthday came up in conversation her father looked at her like she had carried out the first ever good deed of her life by turning thirty on the very day the great footballer died. The man was a big football fan, he never could forgive fate and his wife for giving him two daughters.

All kinds of stuff had gathered in her flat since then, but she still couldn't magic it into a home.

Evening after evening she heard arguments from the neighbours' flat. Four years ago she used to wake to a baby's constant screaming, and these days a young woman was continuously shouting at her nursery-school-aged girl. In the beginning she heard the mother's usual indignation, then thumps, hysterical slamming and eventually never-ending whimpering. She was usually skyping at the time and more than once she was on the brink of going over to the neighbours. 'They're constantly beating a child,' she said desperately to her friend on the screen. Her friend said that you could even hear the shouting through the speakers and advised that she call the police, yet somehow she hadn't had the strength and the bravery. The next day when she bumped into the woman from next door, she seemed surprisingly normal. Her daughter was standing beside her clutching a plush elephant. Watching the strange lady from below with suspicion.

That evening when she sat in front of the computer, the shouting started all over again. 'This is why I'm so alone,' screamed the mother, 'All this! You little crap, why are you sucking me dry? Who do you think you are, eh? Who do you think you are?'

At that moment the Indian man came online. They'd been messaging for three months, he lived in Luton, and he was born in the same year as Kurt Cobain. Ági suddenly decided to give him a chance, after all he still seemed the most normal among all the other men she'd been contacted by. Thirty-one is practically forty, and Luton is practically London.

The following evening she wrote to him that she'd be happy to meet him. The Sikh replied straight away and told her that he could ask for a week's holiday from the firm next week.

At first this seemed a little fast for her but she tried to warm to the idea. It wasn't easy. She looked at the man's funny family pictures, and tried to imagine another life, far from the screaming neighbour and the cold radiators. Sombre men in turbans stared back at her from the photo and serious, dark-faced women. The guy's brother, who lived in Boston, was called Darpan, but she wasn't able to make out from the message what it was he actually did. That evening she lay down on the sofa and romanced about what beautiful Indian children she'll have, while from the neighbour's flat the sound of the little girl's blubbering drifted through.

In the morning she bumped into the mother in the stairwell. She was a thin woman with long hair and a laptop bag on her shoulder. She seemed completely sound, it was difficult to put her face to the screeching voice from the other side of the wall. The child wasn't with her, she must have brought her to the nursery earlier. Ági let her pass in front of her beside the bins and watched as she stepped out into the street. She had a golden pony-tail and a pretty good figure.

That evening the usual show started. 'Who do you think you are, eh? Who do you think you are?' the hysterical voice shrieked, while the water could be heard coming through the pipes and gushing into the bath. During this the Sikh had come online, and let her know he'd bought the flight ticket. She began making plans of where she would bring him in Budapest. She thought maybe they could go on a boat trip, or up to the castle. No way on earth would she bring him back to the flat. She'd be ashamed of the dark room which opened onto the courtyard rather than the street, but more so of the constantly audible evening palaver. She thought of bringing him to Szentendre too, foreigners usually enjoy the little traditional town. And maybe Esztergom with the cathedral on the hill. And to the Gellért baths, though she wasn't sure whether she'd want to strip down to a swimsuit straight away. Had the Sikh left her two weeks for a slimming diet, there wouldn't have been a problem.

Of course nothing came of all this, because from Friday onward the rain poured. It rained from morning to night, dark and cheerless. Her umbrella turned inside out as she walked from the airport bus stop to the entrance, and inside she waited two hours for the delayed flight, soaked to the skin.

Jyran Singh was tall and reserved. Ági's first impression was that he had some aversion to her, but after a couple of days she got used to the slow, slightly aloof manner. Sightseeing wasn't even an option, they had to stay indoors. First she thought she'd invite him to a film in English, but then she imagined taking seats in a small independent cinema with the red turban, and she gave up on the adventure. They ended up in a cafe. It was here, over the marble table, that Jyran Singh presented her with the ornate earrings accompanied by a memorized, barely understandable Hungarian sentence. He was visibly shocked when she smiled and told him that the earrings were gorgeous but unfortunately she'd never had her ears pierced. The Sikh stared at her in confusion, as though until now he'd lived in the belief that women were born with holes in their ears. Ági offered excuses, saying she was really sorry, then on the spur of the moment she told him, no worries, she'll get them pierced tomorrow.

She could have had them done already, but the idea of getting her ears pierced with a 'piercing gun' had always made her uneasy, and she was fine with clip-ons. Now she was determined to please this tall man, so together they stopped in the street in front of the Teréz Boulevard shopping arcade, where the white-aproned beautician looked them up and down with suspicion. The woman ushered them down some narrow passageway past a tanning salon, and they stepped around an open drying-rack with stained white towels drying on it. The beautician asked the man to wait there in the passage while the girl, who would have gladly turned back, was shoved through a curtained door.

As the second ear was being pierced they heard a great clatter from outside. The Sikh had knocked over the towel-rack, and Ági stepped outside to find a hairdresser in rubber gloves resuscitating the turbaned man lying on the ground. 'I was doing a dye and this lad went and fainted,' explained the hairdresser, and the three of them saw the pale man out onto the street.

Unfortunately she couldn't put the new earrings on because she had to wear the little golden stud from the piercing gun for a week. On the second day the hole had already begun to fester and weep, throughout the day she wiped at it with a cotton ball and a reassuring smile. And the Sikh would smile back reassuringly as well, trying not to remember the orange plastic dish he'd seen in the beauty salon. In fact what had happened was that when she'd been gone for about twenty minutes, he figured he'd check in on her. He lifted the curtain and caught sight of a bowl of wax strips towering with gigantic, black hairs. It was as though in the orange dish there were strips of nitty, skinned pig hide. The Sikh drew the curtain and measured his length on the ground, the very moment they were doing the second hole.

The lobes were still weeping after the fourth day, but supposedly the holes were to stop within a week. Unfortunately the Sikh was never able to see because on the morning of the fifth day he left unexpectedly, referring to some complication at the workplace. He'd only left a voice message on her phone which she listened to after work. That evening she sat down in front of the computer in case she might reach him, but he didn't come online. Then at around eight o'clock the usual screaming began on the other side of the wall. 'Well, who do you think you are, eh? Who do you think you are?'

The Fingers' Story

A short, purple-haired woman struggles with the parking metre, picking through her change. She wouldn't usually come into the city centre by car but she has an errand to run. She has no idea how to pay with a phone, plus she can't find her phone, perhaps she left it by the photocopier before class.

Last night she dug the dark blue business card with the silver writing out of her purse and checked the jeweller girl's address, but she remembered the street was here somewhere near the church. The address was the shop's address, her former student is a jewellery designer. She puts the parking slip on the dashboard and then sets off to look for the shop.

She makes to step onto the pavement but there's a couple blocking her path, staring fixedly into one another's faces as they argue. The whole thing takes place without a sound—the young couple are both deaf and dumb. The woman is explaining furiously, flying into a passion, gesturing in front of her face, then meaningfully points at her chest. The man is gesticulating as well, if everything were audible we could say they were cutting each other short. But their hands do scream, that much is sure. The teacher's fascinated as she watches their mime. The couple take no notice of her—they've completely forgotten about the street vibrating around them. They're used to not being heard. Suddenly the man takes a step towards the woman and firmly grabs her wrist. With a single movement he folds her fingers into a fist and closes her hand, as though telling her to shut her mouth. She's surprised, but then frees her hand and continues reeling off what she'd started. She continuously repeats two movements: one of them is as though she was making a devil's head with her right fist, the thumb and little finger stick out, moving it in circles. The other is even more peculiar, as she points her index finger upwards as if warning someone and makes tiny circles. The teacher concludes this is another language, a secret, strange language, and even an argument in it is like some fierce ballroom dance.

She goes around them and continues down the pavement but she can only see a chemist's ahead and no jeweller's. She walks past it twice, expecting to see a window display and doesn't realize there isn't one. There's just a steep set of steps down to the basement shop.

Finally she spots the shop's sign and descends into the darkness.

The girl sees the woman staggering down the stairs but only recognizes her when her hair comes into view. The teacher! She took two whole courses at the language school, after the third she could have sat the exam but she dropped out all of a sudden.

The teacher reaches the bottom and says hi. They'd always been on first-name basis in the language school but now it seems a little strange, she gets embarrassed, thinking it's too familiar. She quickly explains that her niece is going to have a baby and she'd like to surprise her with something nice and unique. Everyone else will be buying her baby clothes, and she isn't familiar with that kind of thing either. She walks around the small shop and takes a look at the glass cabinets on the walls.

The girl's embarrassed too, she lays all kinds of stuff out on the counter on a strip of velvet. She asks the teacher why it's a ring she wants. She adds that it could be a necklace or a bracelet for example, then she wouldn't need an exact size. The teacher picks up the chains, they really are pretty. On the end of one of them is a large ball with holes in it. They were selling these in the cathedral in Toledo, she remembers well because she couldn't buy one. They were called angel-globes.

The girl gets out a bunch of hoops, like a set of keys, so they can find the right size. The teacher says her cousin wears exactly the same size as her, there's no point in fiddling with sizes. The girl jangles with them, showing how tight the ring should be because a lot of people don't know. Her ring finger is a forty-six, the teacher's is a fifty-three. She sets out more pieces and both of them fall silent.

After a couple of seconds, without looking up, the teacher asks her why she dropped out. 'It didn't make sense to continue,' answers the girl, not looking up either.

'A person doesn't learn a language because of somebody else,' says the teacher, and as she's saying it, she knows it's a lie, of course you do. That's the only reason. We learn to speak because of our mother, only for her to never listen to us, never understand us, then we learn foreign languages to continue feeling foreign. The more we learn, the more foreign we become in the world.

The girl says she was only learning because of someone but now there's no point. There was a French boy and it seemed like something might happen with him, then . . . it didn't work out.

The teacher could say a lot on this topic. So much that now she prefers to say nothing and browse the rings, because she really has no idea which one to choose. All of a sudden she spots something under the glass. A big, intriguing, matt-surfaced ring. Angular round the outside, round on the inside and there's something provocative about it.

The girl bends over and takes it out but immediately adds that it was actually made to be an engagement ring, that's what she'd designed it for, but a woman ordered it for her thirty-fifth wedding anniversary, and then she made more of them because she liked the form. The teacher says you couldn't tell it's an engagement ring, and the girl says of course, only she knows, nobody else would guess. And that it's quite expensive, but if the teacher asks for it for Christmas perhaps she'll get it. That's what she usually says at this point, but immediately she feels maybe she shouldn't have: perhaps the teacher's Jewish and wouldn't dream of asking for Christmas presents, besides how does she know what's expensive for someone else.

The teacher says she's completely alone in the world, divorced years ago, she never had children, but it doesn't matter because if she likes something, she goes and buys it for herself—it's never been a problem for her. This ring for instance, she'll take it, and she'll have the necklace for her niece.

The girl stares and suddenly her eyes well up. 'Sorry,' she says, packing the jewels into little boxes, her tears blotch two sheets of tissue paper. 'I'm forever fucking making these fucking engagement rings,' she continues, talking to the countertop, 'and now I thought I'd get one too. Well, I didn't.'

'Me, I'm forever teaching French,' says the teacher. Big deal. 'And just when I think it's worth doing, my best students drop out.'

For days afterwards the teacher thinks about the girl, and the lovers arguing on the pavement. When she got back to her car they'd gone, but she remembers their faces perfectly. After her Friday lesson it crosses her mind that one of her colleagues teaching English was originally a special-needs teacher. She goes over straight away and without any explanation asks her whether she's familiar with sign language.

The colleague is startled, she has no idea how this is relevant now, it's Friday afternoon and there's no time to chitchat about rubbish. She stares up reluctantly from the paper she's marking. The purple-haired teacher stands in front of her, sets down her bunch of keys and starts repeating two signs with a serious expression. 'Totally clear,' says the colleague, and she turns back to her work. 'One of them means forever, always. The other, orphan. Right? Orphan.'

The Vagina's Story

David's lover lays the poppy-seed strudel on a baking sheet. She brushes it, as she'd read, and pushes it into the hot oven and shuts the door. The egg white reminds her of sperm.

She thinks that today she won't let him pull out—she wants to get pregnant. It's exactly the middle of her cycle, it could easily happen. She smiles, winds up the timer and goes out, back to her own flat.

Until now she'd been in her neighbour's kitchen. She has no oven of her own, she doesn't usually cook, never mind bake, she normally heats things up on the hot plate. But today she checked the Internet for how to make strudels, because she wants to surprise him.

The French man loves poppy-seed things. They barely knew each other when he told her that when he was a boy, his mother's friend had baked him poppy-seed crescents.

She was a Greek woman, David mentions her a lot. She always brought him along when shopping with her son. The tiny Marais store was the only place at that time in Paris where you could buy poppy seed legally.

In the meantime the girl returns to her own flat and begins to wonder which position is the most suitable for getting pregnant. Perhaps the missionary. She looks at herself in the wardrobe mirror, then sits on the bed. She has a sudden idea, grabs the four corners of the bedcover and brings it out with the pillow cases to the washing machine —it'll smell nice. The weather's boiling, it'll dry out by the evening on the balcony.

She washes her hair, then opens her laptop, the water from her hair is dripping onto the keys. She's worried that David's written from work, because he's had to cancel several times before. But there's no new message, she closes her laptop. While drying her hair, she remembers that she needs to check the poppy-seed roll. She looks for the keys to the neighbour's flat, but can't find it anywhere. She goes into her room, then back into the kitchen. She's scared now. She dashes into the bathroom and crouches in front of the washing machine. Something is loudly rattling inside the machine's revolving drum. She'd grabbed up the key in the bedcover and thrown it in the wash. She panics, trying to stop the programme, but she can't open the safety lock. The drum is full of water, through the foam she can see the lone key clearly, tossing in the lap of the red bedcover. Meanwhile the smell of the strudel is unmistakably drifting through from the neighbour's, the young woman sobs on the bathroom floor. David has just woken up. He doesn't feel like seeing her this evening. He wants to break up with her, but he's afraid she'll argue with him, and perhaps cry. She's crying now, however, and it's due to him indirectly, but David of course doesn't know. One can't change these things, though your narrator would be happy to do it, especially after this bathroom scene. Fate offered several different possibilities, and reality pointed to the worst one: all right, let's have this one. David knows this eternal law from some-where, and time after time he tries to get round it. But fate is much craftier than he is: perhaps your narrator can be distracted, but not fate. David has no choice between the possible realities—at most he can lay low for a while in the cracks of the stories. He usually lays low in such situations anyway, he simply stops calling. It is nice of him actually, that at ten past seven, he does ring on the girl's doorbell.

We haven't seen her since eleven o'clock in the morning, she's certainly changed since then. Her hair is freshly washed, some light make-up on her face. She's wearing a low-cut white dress, David is staring at her breasts. Oh, I had meant to write, except there was that confusion with the key, this girl has remarkably large, pale breasts and pink nipples the size of tea saucers. It was as though these giant nipples were glimmering through the dress, making David's situation significantly more difficult.

The strudel didn't burn next door, in fact, bordering on a miracle it had baked to just the right consistency. The girl slices it up, David pours some wine. They eat. I can speak in the meantime, so I'll quickly tell you that the woman next door (in whose flat the roll was made) has arrived home, and meant to catch a glimpse of the man coming up the stairs but she didn't manage. She just heard the doorbell.

David speaks about the time when he was a boy, and how he'd like to look for his great-great-grandfather's grave in Cluj. It has to be somewhere,

61

he was called Kozma, Áron Kozma. Kozma, meaning 'burnt food' to a Hungarian, so she can't help remembering the oven, and Cluj—that he could take her with him. Let's trust the end of the story to the breasts. The grandfather from Cluj is resting in a sunken grave. Somehow he survived the hell of war but not Ceaușescu's Kingdom of Heaven. He lived just long enough to hear of David's birth and thought the name David was a bad idea, but his last letter, in which he would have explained that, was never written. Or did I explain this already?

David scans the kitchen. No, that's not quite true—from time to time he tries to take his eyes off the girl's neckline. He suddenly notices there's no oven. He asks the nipples where the oven is. The girl answers there isn't one, then blushes to the roots of her hair. As she explains to him about the woman next door, David suddenly becomes emotional. He's sure she had the strudel delivered or asked someone to make it for her. He almost gets emotional—certainly enough to decide he'll sleep with her after all.

They make love for a long time, we won't describe every detail, just the parts which seem essential. At first David bends the girl over the kitchen table because that's what he usually does, for him it's like a tried and tested opening in a game of chess. Then he reaches under her white dress and checks whether it was really the nipples he saw through it. We'll have to assume it wasn't, that David was simply carried away by his own fantasy, because the girl's wearing a padded bra whose undoing is no easy task. Below she's wearing a thong, which is much easier to pull down, but perhaps he ought not to throw it on the strudel tray. He should toss it on one of the chairs–that's it! Later they continue on the bed and he reaches between her thighs. Her vagina's wet and hot, it almost sucks him in. He moves slowly. She can feel he's going to come soon. Meanwhile her brain has somehow disconnected itself from her crotch and she thinks about how interesting language is. How in Hungarian you say 'to go' and in French 'to come'. She hasn't the slightest idea how significant it is, because the actual situation is the exact opposite, she's just come around to the relationship, and David is going away forever.

The second before ejaculation David pulls himself out of her and turns to the side, taking himself in his hands. It's important to note this because this is how it always ends, without exception. Usually the moment he comes David is profoundly alone. Now he's lying with his back to her, unapproachable, the sperm spilt in his hand. She's alone, too. Soaked with sweat, with an empty and burning vagina, she lies there beside a withdrawn, alien body.

It takes some time for David to return to the present, to grope his way out of his own inner corridors back into the darkness of the room. He remembers the poppy-seed strudel and turns over. He feels for the girl in the darkness. He strokes her breasts, thinking he'll never come here again. He pulls himself closer to her. He doesn't want to sleep here tonight—he's just playing for time. He hugs her tenderly and starts telling a long story. He tells her the story Gavriela told him countless times years ago: how the Greeks came to Hungary after the civil war. Some unknown cousin of Gavriela's lives here, the story is about him. Or, rather, about the loss of words. The girl lies there in the darkness, eyes open as David recounts in a velvety, soothing voice the tongue's story.

CHAPTER ELEVEN, OR

The Foot's Story

As a boy, Peti had always suffered from flat feet. He'd had to practise all sorts of exercises, picking up paper napkins with his feet, that sort of non-sense. His mum took it very seriously. And then when he was eight years old, he had arch-supports made for him. This happened in the January of 1983, he still remembers the day well. They'd had to go to Archer's Street in the Sixth District, and he was convinced this was where everyone came to see 'the archer', whose job it was to re-arch their flat feet. These street names have all disappeared since everything was renamed, but to this day Peti amuses his mum's old friends by calling everything by its old name. It's easy for him, his dad worked as a trolley-bus driver, he knew the whole city.

At the time, when those arch-supports were being made on this since-renamed street, Peti's dad was actually working the trolley which ran by there. His parents had been separated for years, his dad had started a new family and had two new children, but Peti wasn't allowed to speak about this at home with mum. Supposedly the man had met his new wife on the Number 75, so that route was taboo, no doubt about it. On this particular winter afternoon, they were waiting for the trolley, shivering on the slushy pavement, and out of the corner of his eye the boy glanced towards the driver's cabin of the approaching trolley to see whether his dad was on duty or not. He didn't recognize the driver but secretly he hoped that perhaps he'd see his dad on the way back.

They had the arch-supports made but on the way back there was another unfamiliar, moustachioed driver. The boy would have loved it though to randomly meet his dad. He'd wanted to tell him how he'd had to step in liquid plaster cast, for that's how they'd taken a mould of his feet, and how his imprint would stay there for ever now like the people of Pompeii in the lava. He told him the next time they met that he really wanted to see him at work, because everyone in his class knew his dad was a real trolley driver.

When he went over to his dad's the next weekend, they mostly discussed his flat feet. The new wife was against the supports, she said that the muscles in the soles of his feet would get lazy and what Petike really needs is to lose some weight, that'd be much more effective. She made examples of her own children, they've no flat feet, have they? And they never will, because they get enough exercise and they're not overweight. The new wife didn't wear a bra based on similar considerations, because she wouldn't have liked her breast muscles to grow lazy, she'd rather make them work, and work rather hard too. Whenever Peti arrived at their place or left, she would always pull the frightened boy between her enormous, sweat-scented breasts. That evening Peti's dad told her to l-l-l-leave th-that ch-child alone, and Peti knew his dad was nervous, because when he was upset he got an awful stammer.

And he was; that's when his dad decided that on visiting weekends they wouldn't go to the flat any more, but he'd request to be on shift and they'd ride the trolley together. It meant more money so his wife couldn't say a thing about it.

Peti sat in the driver's cabin and felt privileged. Sometimes when they stopped for longer, he got out and came back, so people would see he was with the driver. He liked it most when other children were travelling on the bus, then he'd open the cabin door a few times and look out. Once the poles had disconnected from the line, and his dad had to manoeuvre them back while the curious passengers watched both of them.

In the beginning he was always a little uneasy, because if his dad arrived to work nervous, then he couldn't announce the stops properly. When they hadn't argued at home and he was relaxed, then he didn't stammer so much, but when they had, then he might get a block completely. As they set off, the announcements of the stops would go smoothly because he'd prepared for the first one, but Kmetty utca for example, that rarely went well at first try. Usually it was the names with conso-nants he botched up, especially ones beginning with k, m or p.

It was still slushy winter when his dad, red in the face and worked up, collected him at the final stop for a visit. They were just coming up to the Archer's Street and Peti wanted to tell him how they'd been for a check-up, and how he'd been asked whether the supports were pinching his feet, but his dad agitatedly told him n-n-n-not to s-speak. Peti leant closer—he could see his chin trembling. The first stop he botched up straight away, the second was only successful after several run-ups. At the third stop they waited a while because someone was running to catch the bus and his dad always paid attention to the passengers in the wing mirror. Two boys got on, barely older than Peti, and sat in the front two seats. They were gasping for breath.

They must have run a long way to the bus stop. Despite the cold they were only in track suits, the cold had bitten their hands red. The next stop began with p. Peti guessed there'd be an issue, but his dad dug his heels in and would say it at all costs. He took several run-ups, it was painful. At the next stop it was the same again, only worse. The boys in the front seats were shaking with laughter but Peti didn't catch on straight away. He only realized they were laughing at his dad when the taller, greasy-haired gypsy one began to shriek and stammer the stops.

Peti leant over to his dad and asked, what if he said the stops instead. His dad vehemently shook his head, but after a few seconds he gave a nod which meant, all right, they'd try. As it happened, the next stop was an easy one—his dad would have coped with Hősök tere but Peti now felt entitled to say every single stop from here on. He knew the whole route. The boys got off one stop before the last.

Peti could have bet they didn't have a ticket and he was sorry the ticket inspector hadn't been there, even though he often was on this route. He made a mental note of them and decided that next time he'd ask them himself if they'd punched their tickets or not. If they saw him come out of the driver's cabin they wouldn't dare give him any cheek.

For two whole circuits he announced all the stops himself, peeking back now and again into the passenger area. His dad had calmed down in the meantime, and in his regular voice asked him would he not like to have a slice of cake in the cake shop, it was open until six, he'd pick him up on the next circuit. But Peti didn't want to—outside, the snow was getting up, and the driver's cabin was nice and warm.

It grew dark and the street lamps came on. The snow got heavier and heavier, the ploughs were out and had to drive slowly. At the end of the shift they rolled into Pongrác garage, where the trolleys slept. Normally after a day like that, his dad would take him home to his mum, but first he would give in his papers and say goodbye to his colleagues.

The trolley drivers came in one after the other, they patted and beat the snow from their feet, cursing the weather. They looked Peti up and down, complimented him, saying what a big boy he was, patting him on the shoulder. One of them said you wouldn't even notice the famous flat feet, his own son was much worse. It could be much worse, another said, he still uses supports to this day and it suits him fine. His dad just shrugged his shoulders and in an aluminium saucepan on a hot-plate made tea for everyone, because even though he'd promised Peti back for eight, it was clear he'd absolutely no intention of leaving and going home.

The Hair's Story

It's snowing again, a tall man in a hat and a young blonde woman stroll around the small pop-up forest of dead pine trees. It takes years for this kind of tree to grow to two metres and be cut down. The woman was practically a child when the forest these trees came from was planted.

One of the trees they find too tall, another too sparse. Besides they don't want a regular spruce, they want a Nordmann fir because it drops less. They split up and continue searching about between the rows. Eventually the man considers one to be about right and gestures to her, this one'll do.

'Helga,' he shouts, 'come here!'

'Oh, it's too big for my place,' she shakes her head.

'We always get one this size,' he shrugs, 'the taller the better.'

He's about to add that the children love tall ones but he stops himself just in time. The woman doesn't answer and goes on looking around herself. Eventually they pick out a short, dumpy little tree. He pays.

The seller pushes the fir into the funnel-shaped, clever contraption and it draws a net tightly over the tree. The man lifts the longish bundle onto his shoulder and carries it to the car like some kind of hog-tied hostage. The seller looks on, and claps his chilly hands a few times in his fur-lined gloves.

The man lowers the back seat and slides the tree in from behind. The woman sits in the front and glances down at the compartment beside the gear-stick. There's a CD in it and a hairbrush, full of long, dark hairs.

She has long hair too but she's fair-haired. We can't see it now unfortunately because it's tucked up under her hat, only her fringe is showing. Probably because of the snow, she obviously didn't want it to get wet.

They arrive at the newly built block of flats. In the stairwell they prop up the tree and call the lift. They get out on the fourth floor, the woman lives in the loft space. Suddenly she thinks of last year and the year before, and the year before that too, when she always hoped that they'd be spending the next Christmas together. She watches the man, as he routinely carries the fir through the living room and puts it out on the balcony. She knows that in a second he'll put his arms around her, he'll tell her again how much he loves her, then in a warm tone promise that he'll definitely pop over between Christmas and New Year's.

The living room's already decorated, an Advent wreath is on the coffee table. In the corner is a blue luminous globe now wrapped in silver ribbons. Until two hours ago the woman had hoped that they would have a little time, maybe even make love. She'd put a bottle of dry champagne out on the balcony to chill. She'd been in the bathroom doing her hair when over the hairdryer she heard her mobile ring. All the man said was he wouldn't have much time, and they could buy the tree but afterwards he had to rush off.

Now the woman takes out a tiny package, tied with a ribbon, and asks him to open it specifically on Christmas. If not under the tree, then at least that evening. He's embarrassed and says he planned to bring her present after Christmas. The truth is he hasn't bought it yet because he hasn't been able to get to a shopping centre on his own, but of course he can't admit that.

The next day he means to go shopping in the morning but he doesn't make it. Once again he's wandering about the little pop-up forest of dead fir trees. He picks out a nice tall one. The same seller in the padded bodywarmer draws the net over the fir tree as the day before. Who wonders to himself, didn't he see the same man yesterday with a blonde woman, but he's not sure.

'You're sweet for putting the seat down already,' says the slender dark-haired woman beside the man when they reach the car. They slide the tree in and drive off.

At home he wedges the Christmas tree into the stand. They bought a majestic black pine, the star on the top brushes against the ceiling. The father brings up the decorations from the garage, and then drives to Granny's. They're to be back by five, everything will be ready by then. His wife asks him to buy some fairy lights and angel hair to decorate the tree from the stand in the street if it's still open, because last year's lights are completely gone.

It's difficult to get away from Granny's. She's sick but she's been let out of the hospital for a week, and she insists on the children spending the afternoon at hers. She doesn't want to come over to theirs, she'd rather stay on Teréz Boulevard.

Allegedly she has to defrost the fridge. She's cooked monstrous portions of food, and when her son arrives she's just searching for the tops to all the different Tupperware boxes. She lists what's in what and then spends ages searching about for the gift tags she'd written earlier. The children whine, they want to watch the end of the burglar film at Granny's, so the father decides to take the things down to the car until then.

Outside, it's a cold winter's night, the snow is falling softly, the street is empty. The tree-seller spreads tarpaulin over the remaining trees, propped up against one another, and sets off home, the champagne on the woman's balcony is starting to freeze. The man loads the Tupperware into the boot and remembers the surprise in the glove compartment. It's dark now, it's Christmas Eve, close enough and he decides to open it. He doesn't have to fumble for too long, the ribbon comes undone easily and from the red paper pours a heap of thick, golden hair, cut off in one go.

Terrified, his heart pounding, he wraps it up in the paper again, pulls a plastic bag over it and puts it back in the glove compartment. On the way home, he can't pay attention to the slippery road or the children, his mind is running continuously on the hidden package. For a second he even considers throwing it away somewhere.

When they get home he sets down Granny's boxes in the kitchen and goes back for the rest of the bags. The children are making a din and his wife calls from the kitchen: 'Did you get some lights?'

And since there's no answer, she asks again: 'And angel hair?'

He starts at the word like he'd been caught red-handed and answers almost terrified: 'I forgot. Shall I get some?'

Because if he's told to run and get some, then he'd have another ten minutes, half an hour, a little gap in time outside in the cold air, in the snow-scented night, where the glass bauble of the moon hanging on the dark blue sky trembles, like it could come toppling down at any moment and shatter into pieces. Then there'd be some respite.

CHAPTER THIRTEEN, OR

The Heart's Story

An old-fashioned curtain hung in the seventh-floor window, the kind which is shorter in the middle, like a pregnant woman's skirt. If the readers could fly they'd be able to see into the room. But they can't, so once again the readers will have to rely on me, your narrator, who saw an old woman called Klárika through the tunnel-shaped opening.

Klárika was watching a product demonstration on TV and painting her toenails. It was rather difficult because she was over seventy, but what can you do, sandal season had arrived. On the screen they were showing in black and white all the old pasta tongs and colanders which you ought to have thrown in the bin, and then in colour the new, multifunctional tool which could be used both for draining and for serving.

Klárika hadn't the slightest intention of throwing out her pasta tongs. True, they were old, but they had a red handle, and the red brought her kitchen together. On the other hand, she'd have gladly bought one of these new things, but not for that price. Her head was itchy, she scratched it with a pen because she didn't want to ruin her set hair. Suddenly the intercom rang. Klárika jumped up with a start, wasn't she lucky her nails had dried. That young dear who'd booked for four had completely slipped her mind.

The young woman had been browsing through the list of names on the intercom downstairs for a while when she finally spotted the button with little hearts stuck over it. 'Come on up, dear!' someone said. Ági, as she was called, was unnerved by the informality but preferred not to say anything. She pushed on the buzzing door at the entrance downstairs, called the lift and stared at the warped lino. She got out on the seventh floor, the door was already ajar in the corridor. 'This way, dear!' called the earlier voice. 'Pop yourself down, I've just a couple of things to sort out and I'll be right with you,' shouted the old woman, and closed the door to the living room. The truth was she had left the foam toe separators on the couch and had to hide them quickly.

Ági sat down in one of the seats. Last time she saw one like this was in the children's day-care, they must have found their way here after they were thrown out. She knew the layout of these tower-block flats and made her own way to the toilet. 'You're in the right place, pet, the light's on the right!' called out the voice from before.

A dressing-gown was hanging on the bathroom door and there was a pastry board across the bath. On the board was a cross-stitched cloth and a note reading: Don't sit here!

Ági didn't really understand why anyone would want to sit on a pastry board laid across a bathtub. She would have rather sat on the toilet, but she didn't fancy it any more. The seat and cover were protected by pink terry cloth dotted with suspicious spots. She carefully lowered herself over it and thought about quietly making a getaway after peeing. She was washing her hands when the voice called through: 'You can come in, pet.'

Klárika's agency, the Salon of Hearts, consisted of a run-down computer with a yellowy-grey monitor and a filing cabinet. And of course Klárika, who evidently lived here.

'Your earrings are lovely,' she smiled.

'They're Indian,' replied Ági, but immediately regretted it.

'You've been, have you?' asked the old woman, and began pulling out drawers below.

'I'll take your details down first like a policeman, then we can get to the point,' she said, like she'd forgotten about the earrings. And she obviously had because she had opened the metal box where she kept her money. A large, rhinestone-covered panther dangled on the key-holder.

Throughout the entire conversation, Ági stared at the scalp glimmering through Klárika's sparse blonde hair. It was pink and shiny like looking at the scalp of a plastic baby doll through its nylon hair. To the left of the parting there was a long, dark blue line like a vein. (Your narrator will reveal it was from a biro.) Klárika was chattering nineteen to the dozen, she prattled on, saying that all her clients were honest men, she only ever has gentlemen, she doesn't give out phone numbers, only if the lady patron agrees, and there'll be no harassment here or soliciting fraudsters, because when a fellow pays 50,000 forints that fellow wants something, he's no swindler. 'This here's not like Internetting!' she threw in triumphantly.

Ági could only roughly describe what she actually wanted with some uncertainty, so the old woman rummaged about and set in front of her a clump of photos held together with an elastic band.

'You can have a look through these for a start. Every one of them a true gentleman.'

The first gentleman was a moustachioed butcher-type who was leaning against a Bavarian-style bar as he gawked into the camera. The second was some wrinkled old prune in sunglasses sitting on a yacht and cooked to a frightening shade of black, the third was a lanky, bucktoothed lad with a pit bull. Ági flicked through the photos with increasing speed. Among them was a picture from a work party, a family photo where the two women on either side had been scribbled out, and a passport photo of a stern, sadistic-looking old man reminiscent of a police mug shot. Ági handed over the money hesitantly, there was no turning back. Klárika put it away in a flash, speaking throughout because she could feel the uncertainty:

'Every one of these is an honest gentleman, real sport and travel enthusiasts. Him, the one you're looking at, well, he's actually Jewish, but you know, he included it himself so people would know beforehand in case they had a problem with it. Apart from that he's a good lad. A chef. He's been coming to me for two years now.'

A low-browed, mentally-deficient-looking man stared up at her from the picture. Ági quickly flicked to the next.

When asked what it was she wanted exactly, after short reflection she answered, A nice-looking man who's full of life, with a sense of humour, maybe looking for a family too.

'You're looking for a husband?' Klárika snapped reproachfully. 'Well, don't write that! You'll scare everyone away with that kind of profile! Take your time, meet with each of these gentlemen, then if you like one of them, there's still a chance anything could happen on a sentimental basis. Even a serious relationship! This isn't Internetting, there's no swindling going on here!' she repeated.

She took out another pack tied up with a band. 'These ones,' she added, 'are primarily looking for activity partners, but if mutual affection develops, then marriage isn't out of the question. Occasionally. These ones, in point of fact, are slightly more mature gents with grownup children, but everything is dependent on mutual affection. If you want, I'll take out the bald ones, even though you didn't write it as a disqualifying factor, I just know from experience that it bothers a lot of women.

Well, this one here is bald, for instance, he's been coming for two years, he has. A real gentleman. But it bothers some people if there's no hair. I can't understand where their hair goes after fifty, but that's what happens, my dear. Of course, you're young and beautiful.'

Ági flicked on, confusing trade names flew about the room. Systems psychologist, sector leader, material handler, business owner. There was a definite smell of acetone in the room. Now your narrator will skip ahead, and reveal that later that evening our Ági cried hopelessly for hours and hours, and had dreams of an old woman with a cross stitch tattoo on her head. And she never again answered any calls from the agency's number.

Yet in the present tense of the narration she was still sitting here and was clumsily fumbling through the second pack of photographs. Her gaze strayed onto the ugly curtains, then the carpet, while still mechanically flicking through the photos.

'Now, he for instance came not too long ago, he's a football coach. He was a real professional, a gentleman, now he just does coaching.' Ági lifted her gaze and looked at the picture. Her chest gave a terrible thud, she lowered her hands suddenly.

She recognized the house, the fence, the garden. Until her parents had got divorced she'd spent her every summer there.

Posing in the picture in a white T-shirt and trainers was her dad.

'Do you like him?' pounced Klárika. 'He's a decent fellow.'

'Maybe a little old,' hesitated Ági.

The picture was taken after the heart attack, last spring. Since then her dad had been forbidden from even the slightest exercise and he couldn't go back to the business where he had been working. And Ági knew that never, never in his life, had he really played football, just there at the summer house with the paunchy neighbours. They hadn't spoken for a good six months now. On her thirtieth birthday, when her dad hadn't called, she'd deleted his number from her phone. And later she didn't save it either when he called up and apologized.

'Does he have any children?' she asked, glancing up.

'No. Actually . . . I don't know,' pondered Klárika. Meanwhile she scanned the girl's crimson face, and thought, here's another poor thing who's come to find herself a dad.

The Thigh's Story

'Are we going to the bus stop?' asked the girl.

They had a secret place, the abandoned bus stop. A long time ago, the long-distance bus had stopped there, but since the dairy works had closed, the bus hadn't come around the hill because there weren't enough passengers. Nobody ever lived out that direction. Now an apartment block has been built, and as for the two teenagers, we wouldn't even recognize them if some other chapter were to toss them up again. Certainly not your narrator, after all, all of this happened a very, very long time ago, when the black pine of the future was only a sapling.

In those days behind the bus stop there lay a field of oats, in front of it a black road, quivering with the heat. They always came down here, drawing on the rough concrete wall, standing in the corner and kissing, until someone had taken a shit there the other day. The dog meanwhile dashed about outside between the corn, chasing rabbits or just running in circles, drunk from the drifting smells.

Besides that place they had another secret spot, their own tree. It lay at the bottom of the hill on the far side of the sloping field. It might have come down years ago, but because the machines were able to get by it on the dirt track, it had never been towed. When they had the time, they strolled out there in the afternoons. They sat opposite one another straddling the fallen trunk, and stripped it with their nails. It was enjoyable work, they could pry off big pieces from the rotten top layers. The boy stared at the girl's white thighs as they shifted under her skirt when she leant forwards. Swarming beneath the fibrous strips of trunk were all sorts of bugs. Wood-boring beetles chewed printed circuits into the bark.

'No, I'll show you something cool,' said the boy when he arrived.

The dog was already itching to go. It bounded about and barked, they could barely get its collar on. They had to keep it on the leash at least as far as the main road, because there was always traffic. But this time they didn't turn off onto the small

side road which led to the fallen tree, and they
didn't head up in the direction of the old bus stop
either. They trudged along at the side of the road,
the dog tugging restlessly and sniffing the ground.
Eventually the girl got fed up and let him off.

They caught up with him in front of a green
fence, the dog had its two forelegs on a screaming
little boy's shoulders and was licking his face. The
little boy was screaming hysterically and still
wouldn't stop when the girl put the dog on the
leash again and gave the dog a good telling off.
His mother took the fat little boy in her arms and
hushed him, saying everything was all right, but
he just went on sobbing.

'All right, Peti,' she said, and gave them a hate-
ful glance as they walked away.

'Stupid little wimp, getting scared. Boby
wouldn't hurt anyone. Are you going to tell me
where we're going?'

The pavement had come to an end, they had
to continue on the tarmac. It was a warm July,
now and again their sandals stuck to the tar. The
side of the road was overgrown with weeds,
nobody came walking round these parts. The boy
smiled secretively and walked on. They had been
walking for twenty minutes when the girl stopped

defiantly: 'Cut it out, will you? Boby's going bonkers as well. If you don't tell me where we're going, I'm turning back.'

'Calm down, we'll be there any second.'

The road curved to the left, then branched off, and down the ways it led to a huge, grassy meadow.

Forest belts ran along either side of the meadow, one of them was just a small stretch of parkland, the other was a more serious pine plantation where the darkly rustling black pines of the future grew.

'Are you right in the head? This is it?!'

They dandered down towards the meadow, the girl was sulking and lagged behind again and again, shaking pebbles out of her sandals. It was safe to let the dog off here, so she unclipped the leash. Boby shot off, then ran back, waiting for them to throw a stick. The boy found a good stick and hurled it a good way away. As they caught up with the dog, the girl looked around surprised:

'What the frig is this?'

All around, as far as the eye could see, there were orderly rows of man-sized rectangular holes scooped out of the earth.

'What do you mean?' the boy grinned, 'It was a cemetery. But they started dividing the land into plots, and they had to dig out all the bodies because the families had complained. This place was reeking two weeks ago. You've no idea.'

'No way!' she held her hand in front of her mouth. 'I'm going to throw up!'

'Did you just fall for that?' he put his arms around her, 'it was a shooting range. We passed the no-trespassing sign. Just you weren't looking.'

'Shooting range?' she marvelled, and allowed herself to be embraced. 'For who?'

'Soldiers. When there's shooting practice. But not any more. Now we're going to use it for practice,' he said, and his hand went up her T-shirt.

In the meantime, the dog came back and started nudging them to throw the stick. They threw it, he brought it back. He headed off towards the pine wood, and then he reappeared with a much thicker branch. The girl bent over to pick it up.

'Crap, my hand's all slobbery! Boby, clear off, will you?'

The dog, as though he'd understood the telling off, dropped the branch he'd dragged over and ran off. The boy started groping the girl's breast again: 'Listen, why don't we climb into one of the pits?'

'And what if we can't get out?' teased the girl.

'Then we can stay there, like a shared grave,' laughed the boy, and he started climbing down. She jumped down after him and they were at the bottom.

'We'll only fit if you lie on me,' he said.

They started kissing. He took her T-shirt off first, then slowly reached up her yellow skirt.

'Cut it out, I'm dripping with sweat!'

'Good,' he whispered, and he'd already pushed down her pants. The girl spread her firm white thighs. The dog had appeared at the edge of the pit again. Panting, he gawked at them and began barking madly, as though he meant to save them. She shouted at him angrily: 'Boby, would you frigging piss off? You hear me? Bad dog! Piss off!'

The dog disappeared. The girl pulled her legs together a bit and glanced around embarrassed.

'Something's bloody sticking into my ass.'

She lifted herself up, the boy laid out his T-shirt on the ground for her, then he pulled her towards him. He spread her legs again, then he took out a condom, and tore it open with his teeth.

'No, not yet, please! Not that. Just like we usually do.'

'I want to. Now.'

'I'm scared it'll hurt,' she protested, but she let the boy squeeze in between her legs. As they shifted around, the dog suddenly appeared again, he barked and dropped a bit of saliva on them.

'Boby, bad dog! Go on, fetch! Where's the rabbit? Where's the rabbit gone?'

The pointy-eared head disappeared, the boy searched for the previous position. Suddenly and clumsily he penetrated her and came immediately. They lay in the pit for a while, eventually the girl spoke: 'I reckon I've bloodied your T-shirt.'

He didn't answer, so she added: 'Listen . . . Will you always love me? Like you do now?'

The boy didn't answer, he lay there in silence and stroked her hair, picking out small yellow bits of earth. The loamy sand trickled down onto them from the sides of the pit, their clothes were covered. Above them large banks of clouds drifted past, the wind sent them all one way. One of them hid the sun, and, as though it had swept it away with itself, greyness poured across the sky. They had been lying there for perhaps half an hour listening to the whistling of the nearby pine wood, when suddenly a shot rang out. And then another.

The girl got to her feet, and listened.

'We won't get in trouble for being here?'

'Nah, other people come here too.'

She was rolling her pants up her legs when she turned, startled, and looked at the boy: 'Have you brought anyone else here?'

'Me? Are you thick?'

He climbed out of the pit and looked around, but he couldn't see anyone. He reached out his hand, pulled her up and dusted off her yellow skirt. It was pretty dirty on her bum, but she could go home in it. His T-shirt on the other hand really was covered in blood, on the back there was a big, round stain as though he'd been shot.

'You've dyed it a nice shade of red for me,' he laughed and put it on.

They called for the dog but he didn't come.

'Boby, Boby!'

They searched for a long time, they yelled, then they split up. One of them shouted around the parkland, the other alongside the pine plantation. The meadow echoed in the twilight, but no barking.

They wandered for hours, it was dark and cold by the time they stopped looking. The girl just cried and cried, and he smacked the ground with the leash uneasily. They arrived home late at night. As they walked they whistled, aimlessly, desperately, but only the crickets answered from the darkness. They couldn't remember how they'd got back to the road, but somewhere along the way they lost the leash as well.

CHAPTER FIFTEEN, OR

The Navel's Story

The teacher sat down at the table and began flattening out the dough with her hands. Her plan was that this year for Christmas she wouldn't bake the customary poppy-seed rolls since everyone had had enough of that, but gingerbread instead. There were a lot of children on her husband's side of the family and she wanted to surprise them. She beat the dough flat, then cut circles out of it with a coffee cup. They had no other baking cutters in the house, but with the cup she could still make funny little heads.

The eyes were made of almonds, she pressed in the nail of her index finger where the mouth should be. She made happy faces and sad faces, lining them up neatly on the aluminium foil. The slanty-eyed little faces must have reminded her of something and her work slowed. She distractedly slid the half-empty baking tray into the oven. Out of the remaining dough she didn't knead any more head shapes, she just pressed a big sugar pearl into the middle of each one. She sat beside the oven and absently stared into space. Her husband watched her as she stared, hunched over, and he found her repulsive. A while ago she had started gaining weight, she dyed her hair an unsightly dark shade of red and all day long she barely said a word. At least if she'd had children—but not even that. In fact the only reason he hadn't left his wife was his own incompetence, though he'd been meaning to for years.

But she did have a child, the husband just didn't know. No one, literally no one knew, and sometimes she herself thought it'd never been born, that everything that had happened had occurred in a different time, in someone else's story, and that maybe that nineteen-year-old girl hadn't been her.

After graduating from secondary school, she took a year out, her parents sent her to Nancy to work as a babysitter. Then fate—for the first and practically the last time—offered up various possible stories. But reality pointed towards the worst, saying all right, let's get a move on, this one'll do. The teacher met the boy there, in Nancy, the boy who later never replied to her letters sent from

Hungary via airmail. She passed the entrance exam and got a place doing English and French. The lateness of her period she explained with all the long nights studying and the stress. When it turned out she was pregnant, it was too late to abort the child, she had to defer her first year. Her parents didn't forgive her for the whole nine months, they called her irresponsible, ungrateful and were constantly bringing up her future. They were afraid she wouldn't graduate. Every night ended with tears and slamming doors. On top of that, her parents both worked, they were solicitors, with a negligible affinity for the grandparent role.

Her mum came to the hospital alone and paced the corridor with a grave face. The birth went relatively easily, but when the obstetrician cut the cord at the navel, instead of relief the girl saw the obstetrician's face was strangely harrowed. The baby had thick black hair and a flat, tiny head.

'Mongoloid,' said her mum later coldly. 'You hear? Down's syndrome.'

At the time the girl barely understood her. She lay exhausted on the hospital bed and thought about the words, down, up and down, the ups and downs, this can't be happening. All she could feel was an endless tiredness and some sort of obscure urge that now, at this last moment, she should put right the terrible sin she had committed against her parents and her extended family, that they would accept her back and she could be a child again, that once again she'd be able to lie around on her stomach in her small bedroom with her door closed.

The procedure wasn't complicated. A pimpled woman reeled off some memorized spiel about motherhood, then theatrically reached over the table and took her hand saying she wasn't alone. But she was unspeakably alone: she'd been given one week to think it over and during that time no one uttered a single word at home about the newborn. The baby's navel was still bleeding when she signed the paper to irrevocably give it up once and for all.

But they needn't have snipped the umbilical cord at all, some sort of invisible bond would remain that would never let her forget. In fact, it was as though her mum was doing her best to pull the cord tighter, so much so that sometimes the teacher felt her mum was practically strangling her.

She thought about the girl often and then always counted how old she might be. Five, ten, then fifteen, twenty. She liked to imagine that there existed a mysterious, far-off land, maybe somewhere in Asia, inhabited solely by plump, slanty-eyed smiling people. That her little girl had moved out there and lived in a smiley, furrow-browed man's dumpy, loving arms. And she knew perfectly well that this wasn't the case. The girl was obviously vegetating in some home at the ends of the earth, miles away from the capital. Every time she saw a young woman with Down's syndrome she thought it might be her. And she knew that honestly, even if she wanted to, she still wouldn't be able to track her down, she could never walk over to her and emotionally scan the features on her face, they're all so similar after all, as though they were all related, and thanks to their faces beaming with happy, translucent joy and their jug ears, they looked more like one another than their cowardly, undeserving parents.

From time to time a feeling arose in her that perhaps the girl had died. She knew that this chromosomal abnormality often came with heart disease, that many never reached adulthood. But at the same time she was certain that she would have felt the moment the girl left the world.

About twenty minutes later the little heads were ready, the smell of gingerbread filled the kitchen. She put on oven mitts, took out the gingerbread heads and put them on a dish. They looked a little pale, she hadn't set the oven high enough. On the aluminium foil she laid out the round ones with the pearls, and this time she set the temperature a good bit higher.

She sat stooped over on the footstool in front of it and saw to her surprise through the glass the pearls in the middle of the biscuits melt almost immediately as the biscuits rose into humps. Every single gingerbread biscuit turned out like a round belly, and where the pearl had melted was the empty navel.

'I mean, we could still have a child, couldn't we?' asked her husband from the background, chewing one of the freshly baked gingerbread cookies.

'No,' the teacher answered with surprising resolve, without turning. A silence fell. Next to her head, like a time bomb, was the drily ticking timer.

The Breast's Story

Seeing her now with short hair, almost a buzz cut, he had to admit it really didn't suit her. She had a big nose and her ears stuck out. But back then he was always saying she should wear it short because she had a gorgeous shape to her head.

They hadn't seen each other for seven years, both of them had grown old. No, that's not true. They weren't young when we first saw them in an earlier chapter, it was only that now, everything which had previously just been a possibility had now become a certainty written into their faces. The man drank, for example, and the woman was at the very least unhappy.

They stood in the entrance of the two-storey block of flats, where back then they used to say goodbye. Since then the woman's daughter, who would irritatingly spy on them from the window, had grown into a woman and gone to a town in the countryside to study, and the man's youngest son studied medicine and still lived at home. The eldest son lived with his mother, who had got remarried and who refused to let her life fall apart like those two had.

The man was standing at the window as he explained everything, pondering as he looked down at the garages' roofs. They were the exact same ugly yellow corrugated panels as seven years ago, when everything that seemed to be coming together had started falling to pieces. That's when fate—for the last time—offered several possible stories. And reality pointed to the worst saying all right, let's get a move on, this one'll do. It's always the worst story that gets written into the present, and you can only ever see this afterwards.

The woman was asking about the man's children and took a step towards him. He could smell her perfume: it was the same harsh, melancholy fragrance as back then. And he still wanted her all the same, because he still loved her all the same, or rather love never goes away, no matter how much we bulwark the contrary statement behind sound arguments and gaggles of children.

He turned off the lights because he remembered the woman was shy. But there was still some light in the room, exactly the amount as would have bothered her back then. It didn't bother her, she stepped out of her skirt and pulled down her tights. Then she began to run her hands over him. First his chest, then his nose, because she'd always loved the curve of his nose the most. And he her breasts—he would have reached for them straight away but she was still lying in her jumper. Then she took it off but left the bra on.

Here's a good place for me to stop, because it's true, reality usually points towards the worst possibility, I on the other hand could quite easily steer the story in another direction. But I simply don't have the time to pause for a second. I can't determine which door to suddenly open into that almost obscure moment. His hand reaching behind her back and it's happening here in the now, as you could have guessed. Everything is happening now, in love's ruthless present tense. The hand stops, the bra comes off. At first he only feels the peculiar flat skin, and then he looks. In the faint light seeping into the room he sees that where her right breast should be, there's a four-inch-long, pearly scar with wide stitch marks. And the chest is completely smooth, as though there'd never even been the slightest hump. Nor is there any nipple, just the long, pink, incomprehensible line.

'I'm having reconstructive surgery,' the woman says in a tone, like an apologetic estate agent on a muddy construction site with nothing to show of the promised extras. The man doesn't answer, he just caresses the other full breast, then the scar from time to time out of courtesy. It's easier for him to reach, but he isn't brave enough to touch it with an open palm, only lightly, with the tips of his fingers. Not to worry, he says, it doesn't bother him, her body is still exactly the same as it was, but his whisper is unconvincing nonetheless, because he has no erection, and in a sudden instant he breaks into tears. On her left side he buries his head between her soft hand and her existing breast, and from here onwards he whispers into the dark steamy crack. He doesn't tell her what he's wanted to so many times over the past seven years, but tells her something else. He repeats one single burbled word over and over. It would be good to hear what, but the wet voice is hopelessly drowned out under her arm in the soaking blanket.

On the way home on the trolley-bus the man changes seats. Only afterwards does he realize that it was the back of the seat in front of him that'd bothered him. Someone had cut up the leather back, which had then been stitched up again with big coarse stitches. He sits in front so he doesn't have to see it, he'd rather the litter-strewn city outskirts in spring, the wreckage of the street as it's revealed from under the snow. And he decides to ask his son that evening what they do in the hospital with the parts they cut off, where all those round women's breasts end up. He has to know. He has to be able to picture the breast's last journey to be able to say goodbye to it mentally.

But in the end he's unable to ask his son because he's already deep asleep by the time his son gets home. Although it's not late, it's barely past eleven. It's a pity he fell asleep. To tell the truth, not just myself, but no power on earth would have been able to keep him awake after that many shots of spirits. Moreover, his son would have liked to chat with him, he wanted to tell him that today someone had been brought in and died. He'd performed the CPR. And that Nóra was pregnant, she was going to move in temporarily, at least there'd be someone to cook. He wants to burst into the living room with the news, and that he'd brought the car home in one piece. But in the end he says nothing, because he immediately sees that his dad's been drinking again. He's lying fully dressed on the sofa, the rug pulled up to his chin, his hand hanging from under it, the fingers bent slightly, as if holding something in the air.

The Tongue's Story

Dimitrios hadn't said a single word for the entire journey. He held the enormous worn duffel bag between his legs and slept with his eyes open. His wife and two children had remained at home with family, but Dimitrios had been promised that they, too, would be brought after him within a month. Nakis, who was dozing beside him, had no family of his own yet, though he was twenty-five. He'd left his three sisters and his old parents in Kastoria. All together there were eight of them sitting on the back of the lorry, they had crossed the border in four black lorries in a line, afterwards the lorries lost one another again. There were no children on any of them, they'd said farewell to the little ones two weeks earlier, back at Prespa.

They are dirty, sweaty and covered in lice— the bags are caked in muck from the long journey. Their food has run out and they have to ration their tobacco. During the night they tried to sleep, during the day they looked at the land; the region wasn't bad, the corn grew tall and there was good yield on the grapes.

In the last couple of days the rain had started up, it pattered on the canvas and never stopped. The canvas protected them to some extent but their clothes were wet through. Nakis turned his coat inside out and picked the lice out of the creases. Mihalis, an older man, watched him and constantly shook his head, as though absorbing the rhythm of the Tatra lorry.

After the rain came a fierce, stifling heat, the drying clothes and steaming bodies began to reek on the platform. They were approaching their unknown destination. The sly sun shone in their faces and they lurched in the bends. Everyone's head had grown drowsy with the hunger, the lack of sleep and the exhaust fumes.

It was around midday when they pulled into the main square of a small town. They passed by strange signs written in an unfamiliar language. The Greek men looked at the butcher's, they saw the tall, baroque church and the utterly identical-seeming, impassive women. Locals crossing the square stopped in their tracks, sizing up the

Czechoslovakian lorry with suspicion: it was the third that day. Bone-weary men blinked from behind the canvas, nobody had given them any sign to get off.

Eventually a man in a green combat jacket appeared and loudly conferred with the driver. Neither of them spoke Russian well, so the conversation was supplemented with gestures and volume. They came to the back of the side of the steaming lorry and waved, Come on, let's go, everybody off.

The passengers clambered down, stood with their bags, then set off uncertainly after the man in the green coat. They crossed the square, passed the women watching from the shop window and were herded into a gravelled courtyard. A dog at the back viciously barked at the newcomers until a gangly teenager coming out of the stairwell shouted at it. From then on it just let out defeated whines. It was a mystery as to what the mongrel was doing in a schoolyard and where the actual schoolchildren were. And anyone for that matter, the whole town seemed dead, while the loitering residents seemed so confused it was as though they weren't even local.

'What day's it today?' Joannis suddenly asked.

'Wednesday. Wednesday noon,' answered Marku, who hadn't opened his mouth for days but had kept watch with a knitted brow, always ready to run. He counted the days, counted the border crossings, then under his breath he counted the cornfields and the remaining tobacco. In his head he counted how many cousins he had, including the ones who'd died young.

'It's Wednesday noon,' he repeated sombrely.

Nakis ran back to the gate, he wanted to see whether the lorry had left but the man in the green jacket shouted, ordering him to go back to the rest. They left their packs in the yard and filed into a gym hall. There were Greeks lying everywhere on the floor, mostly strangers. Mihalis recognized a man with a grey beard who was from their area and was even older than him. He was called Zeus, he'd arrived that morning. He said they hadn't been able to wash yet but they'd been given water, and he doesn't know whether they can stay or if they'll have to keep travelling. Most of them tried to get settled so they'd be comfortable for the night, but soon a narrow-eyed man came in and started speaking to them in Hungarian. The one in the green jacket had disappeared.

Nobody could understand what he wanted, they listened to the forty-something, broad-faced fellow completely at a loss. His tone was a shade too firm, and the starved travellers didn't hear the veiled confusion, all they heard was the irritation. He spoke at them for a long time in a clipped tone, then pointed for them to stand in a line. They got to their feet, thinking, all right, the newcomers are getting their water, the whole group was standing.

The man led them through to a large concrete hall whose walls were painted with schoolgirls dancing in skirts and happy peasants bending to work in the fields. In the middle were long bare wooden tables pushed end-to-end into one long line.

The men sat one after the other along either side and took off their caps.

Then nothing happened. They sat, holding their caps, glancing now and again towards the kitchen. Now and again an alarmed woman in a white apron peeked out from behind the frosted glass but not any further. When they'd been sitting for maybe thirty minutes and there still wasn't any water, Marku stood up and made for the door. His manner wasn't threatening, but Dimitrios grabbed his arm and looked him in the eye. Marku silently took his seat and everyone stared at the door.

Soon a short, freckled woman appeared and set out along the tables several spouted, plastic pitchers of some kind of red liquid. She didn't return with any glasses. Mihalis dipped the tip of his tongue into it and said something. The murmur ran along the line of waiting men: 'Not wine.'

The glasses arrived and they awkwardly sipped on the sugary fruit juice.

It was weak and tasted odd but it did quench their thirst somewhat. Some added water from the sink on the wall. Another painful fifteen minutes went by, then a woman in a headscarf appeared and slammed down plastic plates and forks along the table. She didn't look up, she didn't speak to anyone, if there was no space she set the cutlery in the middle on the napkin. Soon after, the freckled lady from earlier appeared with a kitchen hand, a fat old woman, and they shuffled out with an enormous aluminium pot between them. And then another. The two pots were set at opposite ends of the table.

The men began to stir, looking forward to their plate. But the two women didn't serve them, they went back behind the white door and watched from a distance to see what the guests would do. The guests waited a while, then Nakis got up and looked into the pots.

'Pasta.'

Two of them shared it out at either end. First to the older men, then to the rest one by one.

They would have dug in when once again the bony, head-scarved woman who'd brought the plates appeared. In either hand was a bowl of something, she banged them down at the bottom and top of the table and then clonked out again. She was wearing clogs and white socks, like a nurse. In the bowls were mounds of grey dust, there was no way of telling what for.

A few started eating the pasta, others were waiting for the meat. Nakis examined the bowl. He sprinkled a little dust between his fingers.

'Ash.'

'Must be for cleaning the dishes after,' said Marku.

At the other end Dimitrios leant over the bowl and sniffed it.

'Dirt,' he assured them sternly.

Joannis had almost wolfed down all his pasta when the freckled woman and the head-scarved one came out. The freckled one hesitated with a red face, while the taller one raised her voice and started talking in a foreign, glib tongue as if she was furious. She pointed at the bowls and repeated a single incomprehensible word, then made broad gestures with one arm, as if she wanted the guests to leave. The confused men listened and looked to one another, at a loss. She shook her head, then suddenly stepped forward and before they could cover their plates with their hands, she began soiling their pasta with the dirt. On the other side the freckled one did the same, soon they had done all the plates. They glanced back as though they'd successfully carried out their order, then withdrew again.

For a few seconds there was silence, then Dimitrios spoke: 'They've covered it in dirt!'

'They've covered it in dirt, so we can't eat it,' the outrage ran along the table.

Marku slammed down his fork and furiously stared at the tabletop, while the others gaped at their food disappointedly.

'They don't want us here,' declared Joannis. 'Because we don't speak their language. That's why they're defiling our food.'

Dimitrios was so hungry he would have eaten the pasta, dirt and all, but he restrained himself and waited to see what the others would decide.

'We should stand up and walk out!' Nakis slapped his cap on the table.

Support for the idea wasn't unanimous, they hadn't seen hot food for days.

Eventually the old man Zeus stood up, took his plate and holding his head high, walked over to the wall. The others thought he was going to pour it out or just bring it back to the women.

He didn't. He stopped at the enamel sink on the wall, and covering the plate with his big, wrinkled hands he started washing the pasta. The black dirt rinsed off and soon only the wet pasta was left. With that the rest of the Greek men stood up and in single file made their way to the tap to wash their food. The dinner ladies whispered as they watched, nobody dared come out from the doorway.

The Greek men ate, then discussed. As their hunger abated, their bitterness grew. They stood up and filed through to the gym hall in solemn silence. By the time the man in the green combat jacket had arrived they were threateningly lined up in the yard, bags and all. The fat dinner lady dashed out, dragged the man in the jacket inside and pointed in shock to the sink in the dining hall.

The sink was full of scattered pasta pieces while the drain, as though full of greasy ash, was completely clogged with sweet, ground poppy seed.

The Stomach's Story

At this time of night the bus always waited at the last stop, and it usually filled up before it left. The girl landed an empty seat beside a stern-faced old woman, who grumpily moved her shopping bag onto her lap and looked the intruder up and down.

I'm trying to think whether this short-haired brunette character appears somewhere else. Well, does she? The inventory of possible realities is so rich, and the occurring stories either play out before our eyes, or the stories and their characters simply remain hidden. She should still get a name just to be safe. We'll call her, let's say . . . Nóra.

Nóra had been finding it hard to stand recently, but she couldn't tell every person she met that she was pregnant. And it didn't even show, she barely had a bump at all, her blouse covered it. She sat down, scanned the other passengers and then deleted the old messages from her phone. She looked up when she realized the others were watching something. The voice came from the door beside the driver.

Somebody wanted to get on and was shouting as he asked where the bus went. The driver opened the door of his cab and shouted back, Buda. He must have been drunk—he swore, and didn't get on. Finally, when the engine started he climbed on at thse middle door after all.

It was a filthy, half-naked teenage boy. His ribs were showing, he was panting, his trousers hung in bloody tatters. He stood in the middle section of the bus and raised the plastic bag in his hand to his face. He inhaled eagerly, the bag inflated and deflated rhythmically like some kind of air sac. In seconds the bus was filled with the smell of glue. The boy, it seemed, now felt better because he recovered his senses and looked around to see where he was. The bus started and he was met with hostile looks. On a corner he suddenly clutched his stomach, bent double and inhaled from the bag again.

It was impossible to tell where he was injured, but from time to time he cried out in pain, he groped at his groin. Maybe his clothes were hiding the wound, though it could have been higher up, too, but it wasn't impossible to tell because of the dirt.

After a couple of stops he was better. He ran his eyes furiously over the passengers and started to provoke: 'What the fuck are you looking at? And you? You can fuck off too. Fucking scum.'

At this point, I honestly could have got our Nóra character off the bus, any respectable narrator certainly would have done the same. But she didn't want to get off, she didn't make any sort of sign that she wanted to leave the bus or the space of the story. She watched the boy, and when he bent double again she called over to him: 'Here, sit down.'

He slumped into the seat and blinked up at her with suspicion. He took out the bag again, this time he buried his whole snot-covered face in it. He hated this bitch for giving him a seat, and he hated all the other passengers too.

I'm not suggesting the feeling was mutual, but now the other passengers weren't just loathingly watching him, they were watching the young woman who'd stood up for this filth. What's she playing at, is she looking for trouble? The old woman sprang up straight away and clutched her bag as though both Nóra and the boy wanted to rip it out of her hands. She got off but not without giving another look to the two youths.

Nóra almost rode to the final stop, at the top of the hill. At her stop she got off and headed in the opposite direction. She made her way down on the left-hand side under the street lamps, since there were no lights on the bushy far-side of the road. She was just at the crossroads when the boy on the bus shat himself, soiling the already urine-scented and bloody trousers. It must have been something serious because as he lay across the seats he was still clutching his stomach.

He rode until the final stop where he slowly came to his senses. He had no idea where he was but he'd really had enough of the whole bloody city. He set off through the hills, as the crow flies, home to his village. And, by the next day he was home. People asked him how the city was, Well, he said, shit. His mum washed his clothes for him, then at the beginning of the month she bought him a Chinese Puma T-shirt from their benefits because her son had wanted one for ages. A white one those pretty girls would jump at. Well, she had to do something if he hadn't brought any girls back from the city.

That's not how the story goes. He rode until the final stop, where he slowly came to his senses. He had no idea where he was but a kind-hearted citizen in one of the wealthy Buda neighbourhoods took pity on him. He told him you shouldn't steal or sin, son, just because you're a gypsy. Clean all that glue off your mug and come home with me, we have a bit of gardening work, enough for you to sort yourself out. And next time wear a jumper, take a look at yourself.

Sorry, I got it wrong again. I'll do my best this time. So: he rode until the last stop, where he slowly came to his senses. Unfortunately, he couldn't stand up, so he couldn't get off the bus, though the bus driver emphatically requested him to do so. He grabbed at his stomach again, then his glue, and when it was time to start up the bus for the next circuit he was on the floor again. The driver came back with another bus driver, and they deliberated over whether to call the ambulance or the police. They looked at him and voted for the police, saying, The police will call an ambulance if he needs one. Then they grabbed him by the legs, dragged him off the bus and laid him on the gravel. Sure, look at the state of him, that's a crime in itself, seriously.

Nóra, coming round the corner onto the steep side-street, was nearly home. She stopped dead on the pavement, perhaps it was just gas, who knows. She stood frightened, waiting for the tingle to come again. She put her hand on her stomach, and for a second time, she felt the baby move.

CHAPTER NINETEEN, OR

The Penis's Story

Jean-Philippe watched Jyran as he stepped out of
the shower. The chest was wet and hairy. His gaze
slipped lower and settled on the purple, veiny
penis, on the dark testicles, the shiny black pubic
hair that continued upwards in a solid diamond
on the coffee-brown stomach.

The water had boiled for the tea, he poured a
little into the cups. The teabags soaked through, he
started humming the 'It's a Rainy Day' song from
Sesame Street and went about his usual game. He
made the teabags dance like marionettes: they
would press together, then separate again. One of
them lay down in the bottom of the cup, the other
lay on top, then they jumped up and waltzed
again. Jyran had pulled on a blue pair of briefs
and was only half paying attention to the show.
Suddenly he turned to him: 'Why don't you buy
proper tea, you always buy this crap.'

Jean-Philippe fell silent. The impatient tone scared him, he felt something ominous. He added the rest of the water and then milk into the tea and brought a cup in to Jyran. He caressed his back and grabbed the crotch of the blue briefs. Jyran got hard but then unenthusiastically said that he'd just washed. Eventually he did give in, they went through to the double bed, and once again, one last time, they made desperate love. Of course the fact that this was the last time, only we know, here from the distant perspective of the narration. Or no? No, those two in the room knew it as well, that's why there was so much sad determination in them. After Jyran climaxed, he lay on the blanket with one leg drawn up, and to the darkness rather than to Jean-Philippe he mumbled: 'Procreation. Successors. That's what dicks are for.'

Jean-Philippe loved every part of this tall man. The curve of his back, the yellowish tinge to the whites of his eyes, his dark gums and his pink tongue, his white teeth. He loved the playful bluish-grey shades of his curls. He'd drawn Jyran a thousand times, always naked. He'd been his lover for two years, but from the beginning he dreaded that someday the man would just leave him. Not without reason, now this moment had come. Jyran was tight-lipped and determined. He said he couldn't do this to his family, it'd kill his parents. This stuff doesn't happen where they're from. He'd said this many times before, and usually Jean-Philippe just had to laugh it off, he always said this stuff with such loathing.

'Why can't you just say "fag"?' he'd retort.

But this time he didn't provoke, he just sat in the armchair and cried. He said, Jyran couldn't get married, he'd make everyone around him unhappy, including his parents. Jyran answered, what did he know, and moved towards the kitchen. Jean-Philippe suddenly knelt in front of him and hugged him. His head against the blue briefs, but this time he didn't tease him, he rested his fore-head against his stomach and begged him not to go. As though the long-considered decision purely depended on whether that night he'd stay with him or put on his linen jacket and leave. 'I'll get old if you leave!' he made his last desperate argument.

Jyran looked down at him, and tried to take a step back, then said, softly removing his hand from the man's shoulder: 'You are old.'

This wasn't true of course, Jean-Philippe was only thirty-seven, and though the Sikh was two years older, neither of them meant what commonly comes to mind when we say old age. What did they mean?

Loneliness, fear, anxiety, homelessness, which another body can't fix. Jyran Singh had thought of this just now, and of himself, of his own life. He had to go to Luton now, he rented a house there. He set down Jean-Philippe's key on the table without making a show, and they hugged. It only lasted a few seconds: their hips, chests and thighs touched. Their mouths didn't.

The door to the flat closed, and then the door downstairs.

Jean-Philippe went into the kitchen. He fished the teabags out of the trash, pressed the remaining tea out of them, and put them on a white saucer. They lay there nicely beside one another, like on some sort of round bed. Jean-Philippe went through to the bedroom, turned on the light and took out a box. He pressed all the pills out of the leaf, then drank the whiskey from the bottle. He still had the strength to stand up and turn out the light. The light in the kitchen was left on, he didn't leave the bedroom.

It's difficult to place in the sequence of endless stories when all this happened. Every participant would say something different. Jean-Philippe's mother would say, Never: that this whole hazy story played out in the never. Jean-Philippe himself would say, In the always, as it isn't over, it's still going on. The Sikh, too, would certainly opt for the same, though he'd hesitate slightly between the eternal present and never, his gaze staring into the distance.

There, on that irretrievable night he stood smoking on the pavement staring in exactly the same way and from below watched the window that was still lit. How he hated that too: he was never allowed to smoke inside. He thought Jean-Philippe was still where he left him, sitting in the kitchen crying, or on the phone. They'd done this before, that time they only lasted a week, but this time he knew he wasn't coming back. He stood there smoking for a couple of minutes, and when he finished, he stubbed out the butt once, twice, three times on the back of his slender brown hand.

The Tooth's Story

The man opened the door, he was hit by the rancid smell which had set into the flat and couldn't be aired out. He threw his hat on the hook only to forget it that night. 'What a heap of junk,' he looked around.

His mum had moved in to this flat on Teréz Boulevard in 1950, since then it hadn't even been redecorated. It would have been best to sell the flat but there wasn't much chance of that. The neighbours across the landing were selling, from the street he'd seen the advert written on brown paper. Moreover, they still had the old ceramic stove and the frosted glass in the doors, not like here.

Hauling everything out of here seemed hopeless. He sat down in the armchair, weighing up where to start. Since they'd moved the granny into theirs, the cacti had withered in the window and dust lined the shelves. He'd left the fold-out desk on the wall units open half a year ago, when he was looking for the deceased's birth certificate.

Since then he hadn't set foot in the flat, he shuddered at the emptiness and the things which had remained. Towards the end, his mum couldn't even eat. The man, who had fed his children last with a teaspoon, fed the mouthfuls in to her bite by bite. His mum would stare at him confused, then spit out the mush and let it run down her chin. The few mouthfuls she did eat ran straight through her, like through a pipe, and she immediately had to be moved to the chair with the hole in it. Once he had looked, and afterwards thought to himself, there are things you shouldn't see in life. A son should never see his mother's exerting, protruding rectum.

For four years the old woman lived with them, for four years this carried on. Toothless mumbling, then out of the blue, fits of hissing rage. As though his mother had started speaking some colourful foreign language. She joined words together and muttered, like someone reading backwards from a book inside her head. 'You bucketclown cunthorse, you!' she shrieked at her son, clinging to the hospital's white plastic-covered railing.

This happened on a Friday. On that Saturday they went on a day trip to a spa, and the man gave a huge tip to the nurses at the hospital so they'd check in on her.

The children stood shrieking in line for the long, twisting slide. He watched as the two dark blobs slid down the transparent tube, and had to think of his mother's colon. He was worried those two small bodies might get stuck somewhere in the middle. They were out in the chlorine-smelling dressing rooms when his phone rang. He was drying his youngest son's hair with a towel and at first he didn't want to pick up. He did, and he was told that she'd died. The number on the locker was 676. He wondered whether this had any significance—we of course know it didn't. It's always like this. At such times people are susceptible to numerology, they search for connections, they ask themselves what would have happened if they had stayed at home. Nothing.

If the man hadn't taken this trip, he would have happened to be at his lover's on this Saturday, and he would have switched off his phone for a couple of hours while he tried to forget about his own life. In which case the image of his lover's tiny, imitation diamond, letter-H necklace would have haunted him, and he would have thought the H stood for heaven, or hell. But his lover was simply called Helga, and she liked to grip this chain between her dazzling teeth as, straddling him, she lowered herself onto her man. The lover had seen this in a film, incidentally, and thought it would be alluring, but I can't digress now, the point here is his mum's death.

The man started with the clothes. He opened the lacquered wardrobe and took out the moth-ball-scented coats. Laying the heap across both arms he carried them down the stairs to the dust-bins, as though he was carrying his mum's astral body. He threw out the coat hangers as well. Some of them had foreign brand names on them: his mum grew up in a country where these sorts of things were kept as souvenirs. After the dresses came the stripy towels, washed threadbare. The old woman never bought new ones, and if she was given more she passed them on as a present to one of her girlfriends. These he recognized from his childhood. He remembers using the orange one, for example, one afternoon, when he managed to persuade his classmate, a girl, to finally come up to theirs after piano class. They were careful of the couch and they spread this towel underneath them. She had buck-teeth, similar—the man now realized, as he was stuffing the towels in the black bin liner—to his lover's, Helga's. His wife didn't have teeth like that but slightly inward-slanting ones that made her face look a bit like a shark's.

The second bag was now full, and he was wondering whether he'd rather order a skip and hire two men to haul everything out of here, when he felt something hard between the towels and dishcloths. He crouched in front of the bottom shelf and took it out. It was a slender, worn velvet case, originally it might have been for a watch or a bracelet. He opened it and saw, no, it was for a pen. In the pen's place however lay a thin lock of hair. A faded blonde ringlet bound together by an invisibly fine thread. The moths had got at the hair, one or two maggots were lying in the case's lining. Despite the pungent mothballs the flat was full of them, there were even some mouldering away flat-tened behind the glass of the pictures. He pinched the stomach-turning hair. Bad thoughts sprang up in his mind, he remembered a past Christmas when his lover had surprised him with her own hair: it was a sickening, ill-omened gift. He found it hard to imagine that once he had been just as blonde, although he'd seen himself in his childhood pictures plenty of times. Towards the end his mother didn't recognize him at all, which he couldn't attribute to going bald of course but it hurt him nonetheless. Sometimes the old woman leant over to him confidentially, as if to a stranger, and told him about her beautiful boy's blond curls.

His wife and he had never kept cuttings of their children's hair. His wife was a devout Catholic and she loved the relics of saints, but he was totally averse to the idea of cherishing human spare parts as keepsakes. In fact, his wife never let on, but I can disclose that she read something on the Internet about Japanese women keeping the tip of the new-born's umbilical cord. Thus, he never knew but when their second was born his wife had followed suit: she wrapped up the shrivelled bit of skin in tissue paper and hid it in the closet. It needs no telling that the man received no updates on the umbilical tip's eventual fate. He wasn't informed about the bizarre episode when not only did the family cat claw up the closet-floor rug but partook of the umbilical cord too. That certainly would have upset him, so it's a good thing he didn't know.

He queasily rummaged further back because he felt something at the back of the shelf. This was

a smaller metal box, in its time it might have had
sweets inside. Maybe it still did and they'd dried
out. The lid wouldn't come off no matter how
much he forced it. He should have chucked it out
but it bothered him that something was rattling
inside. What if it's a piece of jewellery, who knows.
His lover's necklace flashed into his mind and he
decided he'd call her in a minute, but first he
would go out to the kitchen for a knife. It was
hard to force the top off, it had rusted on completely. Inside the box were tiny, yellow milk-teeth,
some with holes. The collection didn't smell at all
but the man held it at arm's length and put it on
the table. He thought of tipping it into the bag,
then of just tossing it straight into the bin. In the
end he found another solution.

He was standing in the bathroom, staring
down into the scaly toilet bowl when his phone
rang. It wasn't his lover, it was his wife. She asked
how the packing was going.

'Not good,' he answered. 'I'm tired. You know,
I've not a single hair left,' he said looking into
the bathroom mirror. 'Guess what, I'm just after
flushing my teeth down the toilet.' 'Uh-huh,'
answered his wife, 'pick up some bread.' 'OK,' he
said, thinking he'd get some on the way home,

there was a 24-hour shop on Helga's street. Then he gave the chain another pull because one of the teeth hadn't gone down. This time, it disappeared after the others down the blackened hole.

The Chin's Story

Edit and her husband were only going to Dortmund for the funeral, and even for this it was difficult for her husband to get leave from the firm right at the beginning of the year, in February. But the brother-in-law went ahead of them and helped the mum arrange everything.

The father-in-law had died of heart failure in the middle of January. He didn't have a heart attack, even in his death he'd avoided any showy, dramatic scenes, his heart simply stopped. His wife phoned from the hospital—she gave a brief summary of what happened, then added there was no need to come right away, it was too late to say goodbye and she'd take care of things herself. This, it'd seem, didn't go so smoothly, because the day after the death mysterious phantom messages began drifting in from the deceased's email address, as if the sudden death, by way of compensation, had blessed the old engineer with a touch of humour, who then chose this mischievous means to haunt his loved ones. Edit, however, suspected that something else was going on, strictly speaking, that her mother-in-law was incapable of using a computer and didn't know how to send the death notice as an attached file. In reality what had happened was, she'd clicked and clicked through the address list she discovered on the dead man's computer with stubborn determination, generating more and more subject-empty, blank messages, until her eldest son arrived and helped her through this technologically confusing and difficult phase of mourning.

The older brother lived closer to the in-laws— it was much more difficult for Edit and her husband to travel from Hannover with the two kids in the blustery winter weather. She asked her husband whether they should just leave the girls at home, at which point he examined her face from behind his milk-bottle lenses with a troubled look, like he did the treacherous rust stains on the balcony railing before painting it. Edit's husband wore glasses, and every time he had to get new glasses for whatever reason, he always bought the same ones.

Edit remembered the day they bought the first pair, the prototype model so to speak. It happened where they lived, in Hannover, seven years ago in the local optician's, when they still hadn't had their youngest. They stood in the shop, her husband tried on the then-fashionable narrow glasses one by one until Edit said, Those'll do. He nodded, and then brought all five previously chosen pairs outside in front of the shop. He stood there in the faint light of the street, and she had to take a photo of him in each of the five pairs. He then sent the photos to his mum on his phone, and they took a seat in the optician's silver-coloured armchairs while they waited to see what the mother-in-law would reply. The mum was just doing the groceries, she received the message as she was in the middle of choosing vegetables, so the reply was late, but after a good hour they could finally tell the consistently smiley seller that no, it wouldn't be the metal-framed ones after all. Edit didn't want to argue but the chosen pair reminded her terribly of her father-in-law's hideous glasses. Afterwards the mother explained that this sort was less fragile, and she'd know because the old man was forever sitting on his, and frames are too expensive to always be buying new ones.

In every decision she made, she always followed the principle of practicality. For Edit she mostly bought practical household tools at Christmas, like an apple corer, a non-stick baking tin, a food mixer. These went straight into one of the top cupboards of Edit's all-glass-and-chrome kitchen and only came out at Christmas visits. The last time was a good month ago when the grandparents were visiting Hannover and checking on whether their grandchildren were growing at a suitable pace. Edit marvelled at the mother-in-law's rocker-sole shoes—it was as though in the spirit of practicality, the mother had simply integrated her beloved rocking chair, in which she'd ritually sit during Dortmund family gatherings, into her everyday attire. She said her spine hurt so much it was becoming unbearable and she bought the shoes on a friend's recommendation. Now, a month later, Edit wondered whether she'd come to the funeral in them. She could imagine it.

That night she called up her mum in Budapest and told her what had happened. Her mum asked her weakly whether it would be appropriate for her to go to the funeral as well, but she assured her that nobody expected the mum to, they know how busy she is at the hospital. In Budapest, for that matter, people constantly talked about Edit's German marriage and two children as a success story. Her constantly depressed, bag-eyed younger sister lived alone and had slogged through a ton of different jobs. Their parents had been divorced for fifteen years or so, and in the last few years Edit had hardly spoken to her dad, in fact she only called him on holidays. Yet when she was a girl they'd spent a lot of time together due to her mum's constant hours on duty and conferences abroad. Back then, he was looking forward to grandkids, but then Edit had two girls and he had no means of passing on his football knowledge there either, so he soon gave up his expensive visits to Germany.

The whole German family had flocked together for the funeral, as though they were afraid the old engineer might check attendance from beyond the grave. The better half of the grandfather's family had stuck around in the former GDR, and they were standing separately, crowded together on the other side of the grave, as though the freshly dug pit was a negative Berlin Wall, a dark reminder of everything that still separated these people from the other, more fortunate half of the family.

Edit rarely saw her husband's cousins and their harrowed parents but they were somehow familiar to her. She watched them, as they stirred from one foot to the other in their much-too-elegant black cloth coats, bought especially for the occasion, and her own mum came to mind. She knew their features, she knew the arrangement of the wrinkles around the eyes and the mouth, she knew the furrows of silence and anxiety, the well-intended yet hopelessly cack-handed make-up. Every single face reminded her of her own mum, with bags in her eyes from shifts at the hospital, and her desperately struggling, tired skin with its tiny purple veins.

The stony female priest in her black cope strayed to staggering distances while praising the virtues of the deceased, and the children shuffled their feet all the more impatiently and tugged on their mum's hand to point out the interesting bird that had perched in the cemetery bushes. The mother-in-law glanced around sternly and gripped the frame in front of her.

The first time Edit had seen one of these was in Hannover. Back then she was still expecting their first girl, and she remembers perfectly how shocked she was when, sitting beside her husband in the car, she saw three ancient parka coats, like the three sisters of Fate, hobbling towards the zebra with prams. She couldn't imagine someone had entrusted these doddering old bags with babies, and it was only when her husband slowed down and let them pass that she realized these old bats weren't pushing prams, they were pushing Zimmer frames with wheels.

It was on one of these wheeled contraptions at the very front that the mother-in-law was leaning, her chin pinned to her chest, enveloped in the cold breath of martyrdom. But her chin wasn't pinned to her chest, that's not quite how she was holding her head because the button of the old woman's chin was in fact missing. The part below the mouth sloped sharply towards the neck in a curve lacking any cartilage, and as a result the granny wore a permanent look of slight offence.

Edit had realized her husband had no proper chin either when he first trimmed his blond but quickly greying beard. That's when it became clear her mother-in-law's stern squirrel-face was not only recognizable in his older brother's face, as Edit had always noticed, but in her own husband's too. On the right-hand side of the grave, it was easy to recognize the mother-in-law's descendants, because all of them, to varying extents, bore these genetic squirrel features in their sloping chins.

The sun was shining over the cemetery, but it was getting colder, and death's blond-eyelashed priest wasn't quite managing to find her way out of the otherwise not-too-complicated, one-way labyrinth that was the deceased's life story. The relatives were getting cold, they rubbed their hands, while at the granny's signal, the little girls, bored stupid, sidled over to flank either side of the walking frame, and shuffled from foot to foot in their woolly tights.

Edit watched them from a distance. Their eyes were a sharp blue, seemingly both of them had inherited their Budapest granny's eyes. Their wavy hair resembled Edit's, and their face their dad's. Your narrator saw it the same way and, what's more, your narrator knew all of the nice and good things which the mum was now compiling an inventory of in her head. Namely, that the girls were good singers, that they had an extraordinary sense of rhythm and were promising counters.

The mother looked at the profiles of the two little pale faces in front of the black background of the freshly dug pit, and discovered what your narrator had spotted a long time ago and what the relatives standing on the far side of the grave, who rarely saw the girls, had all by now quietly ascertained. The charming girls had no chins, and they plainly, unequivocally belonged to the squirrel-heads.

The Sole's Story

For a minute it was as though the woman were asleep. No, it's not David's girlfriend lying there with her eyes open, listening to the man's velvety voice, it's a somewhat older and thinner woman of about forty.

Her neck begins to feel stiff, so she turns her head to the other side. The towel pressed into her cheekbones, she turns her head and now the reader can see her. It comes as no surprise if you don't recognize her, we've only met her once and she was wearing a winter coat. The massage table is uncomfortable, lying on her stomach, as she is, she has nowhere to put her head. In the middle is a hole to dip her face into for her own comfort. It's a hole for crying into, she thinks. Not for comfort, for crying. She thinks of swimming lessons back in the day, when she had to dunk her head in the water.

From time to time, the masseur asks whether it hurts, then goes on speaking about all these chakras and reflex points. She isn't listening again—tied down with thoughts.

She has a slim bony body and a straight pointed nose. She's tied up her dark hair so it won't get cream on it. If she wasn't lying on her stomach we would see that she had lines across her skin from the pregnancies, and her breasts did rather sag. Though to be fair, when she's dressed she looks all right.

She began coming in for foot massages two years ago, essentially because of migraines. The migraines had disappeared since then—in fact they disappeared this January when her mother-in-law died. She had been unwell for eight years and spent her last months in the hospital, but before then she lived with them in their flat for four years.

The bouts of headaches started when her husband had his mum moved in. The old woman would spend the entire day sitting on the couch, either dozing or dealing out orders. She didn't l ike anything they cooked and nothing ever put her at ease. She kept her walking stick by her side, and when she wanted something she'd bang it on the floor furiously. She argued with long-dead acquaintances and yelled at the children when they came home from school. She sat there glowering, resentment and the smell of pee seeping out of her, while behind her head, a large, dark stain spread across the wall. It has since been painted over during the renovation, but sometimes when the woman looks at the wall she imagines she can still see it.

The masseur asks again if it hurts, then begins pressing the soles of her feet so hard it's as if he wants it to hurt. Supposedly he can feel knots in the middle.

Still, she enjoys it. She was on her feet all day long. She had to unpack everything and put it back in the cupboards and unpack the children's things. Luckily both are at camp now, so at least she doesn't have to cook. Her husband is busy with his mum's flat, it has to be emptied out for renting. It's a nightmare, but thank God it's not up to her.

The masseur is talking about some seaside work that he was almost scammed into and, fair enough, it was a good thing he hadn't taken it. The deal was he could holiday there for free, he just had to give massages on the beach and hand over a cut to the owner. A mate of his actually went but came back saying the whole thing was a load of crap and the chinks had a monopoly on every beach. Eventually he found work but it was crap, he had to pose for pictures in a costume with little kids on the beach. Who'd enjoy that, eh? Wouldn't you rather just go to the lake?

Yeah, replies the woman. You don't have to accept everything. There are things you can live without. There's something else entirely she wants to talk about but she doesn't have the guts, not even like this, staring at the floor. She wants to say that her husband is leaving her. When she's finally worked herself up to talking about it, the man sprinkles some talcum powder on her feet and tells her they're done. The woman slips into her shoes and pays.

When she arrives at the flat, she completely forgets about the talcum powder and leaves floury prints behind her on the freshly polished parquet floor. She turns on her phone and calls her husband to ask him to get some bread. She's not in the mood for conversation, she knows he meets with that little slut every Thursday.

The woman also knows the little slut is called Helga too. If she wanted to, she could call her. But she doesn't, she switches the phone off.

Now where's she gone? She's suddenly disappeared from the living room. Let's follow the white footprints!

She's gone into the granny's room, which of course isn't the granny's room any more. She wants to see how it looks all empty. Whether she can see the stain or not.

She goes in and turns towards the couch. Above the back of the couch she sees a dirty grey circle looming. Where the head would be. She switches on the light, steps closer and looks again. Nothing. She puts out the light, goes to leave, then turns around—it's back again.

She puts on the light a second time, steps closer and looks up at the ceiling, at the dated globe lamp. All of a sudden she bursts out laughing and switches the light on and off. When she turns it off, the glow of the streetlights outside casts a faint shadow of the globe lamp on the wall, just above the sofa, about where the granny's head used to be. The shadow also has a thin stem but it's barely visible. It's as if the whole thing was some bad joke played by the dead granny. The woman laughs at the joke, a little too long perhaps— it's not that funny. She sits down on the sofa in the dark.

A few minutes pass, her sitting in the granny's seat. She thinks about how pointless these fucked-up four years with the old woman were now that her husband is leaving her. He couldn't do it while they were here looking after his mother. But he'll do it now because this Helga girl won't wait any longer.

She feels dead tired and can't remember whether she actually phoned about the bread in the end or just meant to. Suddenly, something occurs to her. Everything becomes so clear and simple that she jumps up bursting with energy.

She goes into the pantry to get the strap that the workers had used to move the wardrobes. There it is in a basket, fairly grubby. Doesn't matter. She goes into the bedroom and pulls the strap through the highest of the bookshelves they'd drilled to the wall. She checks to see if it'll hold, even though for the children's sake, she'd specifically asked the workers to fasten it well. The little aluminium ladder is still standing there from when she was putting the books back up that afternoon. She lines it up carefully, smiling mischievously the whole time like someone who's managed to muster up a joke even better than the granny's. It also occurs to her how often her husband uses that expression, that somebody has both feet firmly on the ground. Well, this Helga, for sure she's just that.

She stands up, crosses herself, and kicks herself away. One of her legs reaches out frantically for support on the round top of the stepladder, then slips to the side. The other kicks about as though somebody was tickling her in the air.

Her husband doesn't get home until after midnight. He lets in the cat, annoyed that it was still outside. He takes off his shoes and marvels at the white footprints on the parquet flooring. The light in the bedroom is on, he goes closer. He can't see the rope through the door, the first things he notices are the two soles of the feet, then the smell of pee. In this position, the woman seems even thinner. Above her, the freshly painted ceiling is strewn with deep scratches.

The Mouth's Story

David got another message from the firm, in which a man called Besnik promised him samples and apologized for falling behind a couple of days. He still hadn't given a telephone number, so David couldn't call him to give him an ultimatum. The price quote given in English and riddled with amusing translation mistakes explained that besides medical silicon products the firm also manufactured polyamide, polyester and polypropylene products, as well as Lurex-based surgical materials, all produced to outstanding quality of course and using cutting-edge technology. The firm's head offices were actually in the town but, to judge by their website, a great deal of their products were manufactured in a place called Botoşani in northern Moldavia due to cheaper labour there. David thought he might need to verify Botoşani's cutting-edge technology and Googled all the information he had regarding the firm. After a little searching

it turned out that they also manufactured mod-
estly priced inflatable dolls with a skin texture
that felt natural to the touch and which came in
three different hairstyles. From there it was only
one or two clicks till he was led to the rather enter-
taining websites of rubber-doll collectors, and to
Romanian sex toy manufacturers.

David had waited four days in the hotel for
the firm's representative to get in touch, so they
could perhaps sign a contract with the Bucharest
clinic. He didn't have much faith, he wanted to
leave on Saturday and if they didn't manage to
negotiate by then, he wouldn't contact this sup-
plier again. On top of that they had no references,
and he didn't want any malpractice court cases for
inflamed silicon breasts.

By the afternoon he was tired of sitting in front
of the TV screen, he decided to go out for a stroll.
The town wasn't big, he'd already walked the
length of the more important streets and always
ended up at the little square on the edge of town,
where every evening, lingering in the stucco doorway of a beautiful building marked for demolition,
a chilly-looking prostitute shuffled her feet. At first
David had taken her to be a scrawny child, as she
shuffled about on her spindle legs in platforms. He
didn't see her face, it wasn't until the next time

when he got a better look and discovered to his horror that she had a harelip.

David had seen more than enough corrective surgery to understand the symptoms of the cleft lip and the problems that came with it. At first glance she seemed a serious case, and as a surgeon he wasn't sure whether she could even articulate or speak, in other words whether her palate had been repaired. Only the most extreme poverty and desperation could have driven her to stand on the street with that. David couldn't get rid of the thought she might offer oral services to clientele susceptible to curiosities.

It was past seven o'clock when he crossed the bridge and arrived at the small square. She was standing there. She'd seen him come by this way several times already, because she coquettishly glanced up at him and took one or two unsteady steps towards him. She had the young, unripe face of an adolescent, but her eyes were sensual and tired. David was scared she might approach him, so he turned hesitantly and headed back along the riverbank.

The next day he got a message from the Besnik man that he'd bring the implant samples and all their references, that he'd be in the town by the evening, and to please accept his apologies, but the rain running down from the mountains had caused a lot of chaos, he hadn't been able to make it up from the countryside until now. David wondered, how that was possible, wasn't this the countryside, and was relieved he wouldn't have to stay any longer. He set off on a light morning stroll. At this time of day he never went further than the hotel's neighbourhood. But now he was suddenly struck by the desire to repeat last night's route, and he soon ended up at the familiar little square. He was surprised to see that she was standing there again, but without a coat. In the daylight she seemed even more of a child and paler, and of course she straight away spotted David approaching. She looked at him and stuck out her long pink tongue licking the rim of her split mouth. David was shocked to feel the excitement rush to his crotch and quickly turned his back. He automatically paced uphill, up a street towards the modern, uninteresting, dirty part of town he'd never fancied clambering up to. He'd been walking for about five minutes, his heart pounding, before he finally dared to slow down. He was surrounded by shabby tower blocks, he could see shops and a half-completed building. He didn't want to go back the same way because he'd end up on the square, so he turned left to reach the centre via a detour.

As he stepped across the potholes in the at times impassable tarmac, he suddenly noticed something quite peculiar. I will try to describe it accurately, but it's tricky because I have to include David's perspective, who was examining every single detail around him with the buzz and suspicion of a foreigner.

Behind a glass shopfront was a line of white, reclining chairs, and the walls inside were lined by mirrors. On one of the reclining chairs lay a girl, but he could only see her hair. A small white cloth held back her hair, which poured out from under it in brunette, shining swirls practically reaching the ground. A woman in a white coat was bent over the girl's face like a dentist. Her head moved rhythmically up and down like a pigeon's, and she was holding her hands up in the air. It looked like she wanted to kiss the girl but couldn't reach her face because some sort of force was rhythmically tugging her back. David couldn't imagine what was going on. The woman's head went up and down, every now and again adjusting something on her out-stretched hands, but she never bent lower than a certain point.

She must have felt she was being watched because she looked up. At first confusion and anger showed on her face, then naive curiosity. She lowered her hands and smiled. She must have said something to the woman lying down because the cascade of hair moved as well and the second woman sat up in the chair.

David had never seen a more beautiful face in his life. He stared and stared, so captivated and confused that this second woman broke into a smile too, and through the glass she clearly mouthed something. Then she shooed David away with her hands, he held his arms out to explain he didn't understand, and waved for her to lie back down. She lay back and the other woman started the pigeon head-bobbing again.

There was a sign displayed above the big glass entrance, it was an exclusive hair and beauty salon. It was only much later and with difficulty that David managed to understand she'd been plucking the girl's eyebrows. In her hands were two crossed invisible threads which she pulled with her mouth and guided with the motion of her head. The girl's upper lip and face had to be done as well, so she was pretty surprised when she was done a good twenty minutes later and saw David hanging about at the end of the street.

The girl, and he didn't need to lip-read this time, was called Nazeli. Anyhow she could have been called anything, David could hardly breathe, he couldn't get enough of how improbably beautiful she was.

Everything about Nazeli was perfect. Her supple white-skinned body, a bum like an upside-down heart, her heavy shining hair, her arched jet-black eyebrows. And her mouth! She had a plump, deep-red, laughing mouth, and the smattering of French words fell clumsily from her lips. She didn't need many because from what little she'd said, he understood she was twenty, worked in a shop and the beautician was her friend.

The next week David woke up in Bucharest, and she was blinking beside him. David grabbed her breast, ran his hand over her full downy thigh and penetrated her again. He became entranced as he moved inside her, inhaling the smell of her hair, which sometimes reminded him of peaches, and sometimes the smell of grass. Suddenly, in the seconds before coming, from somewhere deep inside him the face of the hare-lipped prostitute flashed into his mind and, losing control, David came between Nazeli's legs. Then he lay limply on top of her, staring at her opening lips. He could see the little dark hairs beginning to show above her mouth, and thought even that suited her too.

The Gum's Story

Gergő showed the guests up to the first floor. In the wine cellar's newest wing was a room expressly designed for tastings. From the wide panorama windows you could see the sloping vineyards of Villány. There was hardly a leaf left on the vine-stock but the late autumnal landscape still looked beautiful with the low clouds and the limestone terraces. Gergő had come to love this part of the country. In spring he'd moved down from Pest for the new job. The house had been bought cheap from an engineer's widow. The lady wanted to get rid of it quickly, and it didn't need any fixing up at all because the bloke had painstakingly restored it himself—supposedly he worked in the preservation of monuments. It was a lovely little house with a porch and iron-fitted windows. They had even left the furniture and the coarse woollen throw with the embroidered pillows.

Gergő held his glass up to the light and began explaining: a dark ruby hue, a colourful, complex bouquet, with characteristically warm tones. In the mouth it gives a balanced sensation, the tannins are exquisite. It's worthwhile taking your time as you swill and turn the wine in your mouth. When he got to this bit his phone suddenly rang. He would have said, I'll call you back, but he saw on the screen that it was Anó. Anó was his granny, he'd called her this as a child and then somehow the name stuck in the family.

'Well, guess where I am, Gergőke.'

Anó asked with such excitement it was as if she was calling from the Moon. There was nothing he could do, he had to take a step aside and listen. Anó was standing on Teréz Boulevard of all places with Uncle Gabi in front of the building where she spent her childhood—right until '45. She was the only member of the entire family, by the way, to survive that childhood: her three siblings had been killed in Treblinka, as had her parents and grandparents. Uncle Gabi, Anó's second husband, had lost every one as well but they didn't speak about that. The old man had never seen this Teréz Boulevard building, in fact he'd always lived in the wealthier, Buda side and only for the most justified reasons was he willing to cross the river and go over there, that is, to Pest. This time the reason seemed justified, he had to go with Anó to the dental technician's. In the last few years, all of her teeth had fallen out due to receding gums, despite the mouthwash and all those injections. She could not walk around without any teeth, could she, but that doctor on Böszörményi Road had gone and died on her before her new set was ready, the brute. 'Oh dear, that's a pickle,' Uncle Gabi concluded about the situation, and got her an appointment with his friend Klárika's dentist who unfortunately had his surgery over there. He wasn't fond of Klárika herself though, and was always referring to her as the madam of the brothel, still, he had to acknowledge: her teeth were in good shape.

On the way home from the dental technician's (Klárika was right, he really was quite the gentleman) Anó and Uncle Gabi were passing by the building, and looked up at the second floor. There was some brown paper stuck across the window with For Sale written across it and a telephone number.

'Give it a ring!' said Gergő to buy some time. 'Sorry, but I really have to go, we've got guests.'

Uncle Gabi called the number and the owner answered saying he happened to be in the flat, so they could come up. A girlish stage fright came over Anó, she dawdled about in the stairwell and looked at the names on the letter boxes. She couldn't find many of the old residents but the original tiles were still on the ground, and on the first floor the same frosted patterned glass in the swing door as before. Anó remembered how the neighbours across the way had broken the other half with a floor lamp when they moved in in 1950. Uncle Gabi thought paying a visit was a very bad idea but Anó insisted they go up.

An overweight, balding man opened the door. He was wearing a padded jacket because there was no heating in the empty flat. He invited them in and as they stood in the entrance hall he started explaining why it was good to live in the centre of town, especially for older folk who, naturally, don't like making long journeys if they have to run an errand. Uncle Gabi nodded with a vacant look, Anó started through the double doors into the next room, stopped and looked around. The tile stove was still there, and although the walls must have been painted at some point, nobody had touched the doors in ages. They were yellow, worn and stained. The parquet flooring creaked, they hadn't redone it either. She could see some lines on the door of the smaller room at the very back. Anó went closer and bent over. She knew whose mark was whose: the topmost line was her own at four-foot-nine, and the lowest one under the door handle was her brother's. The old woman couldn't take her eyes off the scratches until Uncle Gabi put a hand on her shoulder.

'This is where the grandfather chair was,' Anó pointed to the corner, her voice shook. Their mother had always sat there to read to them, or when she was telling stories of her childhood, about Cluj. They'd found the armchair since, a bit grubby, after the war. One of the neighbours had taken it in, like the nuns had taken in Anó. Later it was re-upholstered and Gergő's dad inherited it. And last year when Gergő moved from his parents' to the countryside, that was the one thing he'd taken with him from the family furniture. Not for himself but to please his granny. He positively hated the armchair and never sat in it.

In the hall the owner was relating the conveniences of the flat's orientation when Anó excused herself and tottered out of teh front door to make a call. She considered mobile-telephone calls ill-mannered, as though she was powdering her nose in the company of others. She stopped in front of the wide shiny stairs and keyed in the number.

'Gergőke, tell me, do you remember the story I told you about the armchair?'

Gergő very much remembered, she'd told him a hundred times. On top of that Anó had a lisp now because of her teeth, it was painful to listen to her. The wine-tasting guests were just being served sandwiches and cheese, which was a good excuse for him to leave the reception room for a bit and go through to the kitchen. Every time Anó had read to him as a boy she told him how his great-granny would come and sit in the children's room each night, and he'd heard the family anecdote about his dad a million times.

In terms of choosing when to be born, Gergő's dad wasn't much better than the granny: he chose to arrive into the world on the exact autumn afternoon when the Russian tanks were shooting the neighbourhood to pieces. According to the story, his father had been one year old—Anó never failed to share this story with the family—when the local paediatrician was transferred to the countryside. Some young man arrived in his place, and when he leant in to Gergő's father with his stethoscope, the boy sat up in the grandfather chair suddenly and began eyeing up the stranger. The doctor bent over and the boy groped at his face and moustache. He touched it for a while, then in a throaty voice he gurgled: Goy-Goy-Goy.

Gergő was afraid Anó might tell him the whole stupid saga for the thousandth time. It wasn't funny the first time, but the hundredth time round it was categorically painful. Luckily that's not what followed but, instead, a detailed description of the tile stove and a list of the names of residents who were still alive.

'I'm sorry, but I have to get back to the guests,' he cut his granny off. 'They're waiting for me. You know, I've a wine tasting.'

Gergő hung up and thought he might as well turn the bloody phone off. And sell the grandfather chair, that's if anyone has any use for it.

Meanwhile Anó went back into the hall where uncle Gabi was following the owner's movements with a resigned look, 'That there's a main wall, and that one too, the other two are thinner,' said the man, 'I'll show you the toilet and bathroom as well.'

'Allegedly,' he continued, entering the echoing bathroom, 'There used to be Jews living here. I mean, I don't know how much is true, but when I found out I turned the place upside down. I opened up the drains and took apart the air vent as well in case they'd hidden their gold there. But I didn't find a thing. I didn't take the parquet up though, it might be there. If it is then you'll have got yourselves a good deal,' he grinned.

Uncle Gabi's gaze was fixed on the tile joints, Anó's on the window which opened onto the light shaft. If she'd been able to think, she would have noticed how dirty it was. But she couldn't, the words had gone from her head. She stared into the murky space which had appeared as if from nowhere, like back in the day when she'd stare down the light shaft at the rotting dead pigeons.

In the meantime, Gergő had returned to the table and was filling the glasses.

'This year has done particularly well in comparison to previous years of the same wine,' he recited. 'A thick robust wine, warm with hints of cherry. A deep ruby colour. Take a look at it, it's as thick as blood. A character of mature tannins and complex ornamentation, with a lingering aftertaste, verging on the bitter.'

The Nape's Story

The man sat in front of the screen and watched the footage for the umpteenth time. It was effectively useless. He couldn't find a single clip which would fit the preliminary concept, or would at least be amusing. It'll not work, he thought, he'll get nothing out of this. But the advert had been up for four days outside, it should have worked.

It seemed like a good idea when he first got into the whole thing. He'd stretched a huge white poster under the first-floor window, the kind that estate agents would put up. On it was written in red letters THIS FLAT IS NOT FOR SALE. Below were a telephone number and an arrow which pointed directly to the front door. The idea would have been that people only read according to their desires, meaning whoever does turn up wants to buy a flat. He wanted to shed light on the fact that in reality people don't see what's in front of them, and that people can only assess and reassess unfamiliar situations one step at a time, before they put together the details and see the real picture. He imagined how he'd sit the enquirers down, give them a tour and explain them why this flat is not for sale, why no sum of money would part him from this quaint little nest in the heart of London. His gallery director was delighted with the idea, he hugged Jean-Philippe and wanted to see the finished project by the autumn.

Jean-Philippe smiled to himself when he collected the banner—he really should have got the poor lad from the shop on film as well because of how he protested. Jean-Philippe regretted not bringing his camera. Then he began fantasizing about how he was going to cut the enquirers' faces and in what kind of context he'd exhibit the finished film and the banner. Maybe he'd put a ground plan of the flat alongside it. Perhaps a couple of photos of the rooms as well.

On the first day nobody came, not even a phone call. Not to worry, he thought, it'll take a while for the passers-by to register the advert. It's not a high street, the only people passing by are people with homes here.

The second morning the entry phone finally rang. He set up the camera, went over the speech in his head and opened the door. A black couple stood gormlessly in the door. The man's hair was turning grey and the woman was awfully fat and haggard. They insisted on taking off their sandals, then stood in the living room unsure of what to do. It took some time until he sat them down in the right places and he could start into the speech.

The black couple smiled readily and didn't want to take the tour, they were politely silent. Now and again Jean-Philippe double-checked with a question, and they would look at each other and nod, as though they were giving their considered consent for something. In Jean-Philippe the initially faint suspicion grew ever stronger that perhaps the married couple didn't speak English. All of a sudden they pulled a wad of cash out of a plastic bag, held it up to him and smiled again. When he asked whether he should turn off the camera, they agreed enthusiastically, and when he asked whether it'd bother them if he continued recording their faces, they nodded in unison once more, of course, of course. A strange anxiety and a foggy feeling of shame came over him, so he stopped recording and put on the kettle. The married couple poured themselves two cups from the boiling-hot teapot, gulped it down, filled another, gulped it down again, and carried on sitting motionless on the sofa. It was as though they thought the tea had marked the closing of the sale, and they were waiting for him to quickly gather his bits and be off. Jean-Philippe started to sweat, and to buy some time he started repeating next week, next week. The couple must have been sent away plenty of times already by plenty of means, because they stood up immediately. The whites of their eyes were yellow and their bare feet were wrinkled as though they were wearing tights.

When he watched the footage back, it struck Jean-Philippe that the man's purplish dark lip had trembled as they made their way out.

Then nobody came.

On the fifth day, by which point he wasn't counting on anything, the entry phone rang again. A group of visibly high boys squeezed into the room, immediately sat down and stared at Jean-Philippe with an enquiring look, as though they'd happened upon some restaurant terrace and he was the waiter. As a set-up it wasn't bad, in fact, it seemed useable. He went out into the kitchen to bring them something, while one of the boys had already started rifling through his CDs. Meanwhile he turned on his camera and started filming them—not a word was said about the flat. Two of them went through to the bedroom and lay down on the double bed fully clothed, while a third boy lit up in the kitchen and enquired about some Robert guy, whether he'd been here or not. He spoke bad English and simply wouldn't understand that he couldn't smoke here, so he stared in surprise when Jean-Philippe finally took the cigarette from his mouth and stubbed it out in the sink. The boy looked at him with gentle, velvety eyes and repeated this Robert name again, before seeing off a fearsome amount of ravioli and turning on the TV.

The others had somehow got themselves together and were getting ready to leave, but the guy lounging on the sofa had nodded off. They called to him, then shrugged and left him behind.

Jean-Philippe got the camera and filmed the boy's face. So his name was Imi. He had thin, bluish eyelids and long eyelashes. He slept curled up like a child, his long hair hanging in his face.

When he woke up hours later, he coolly asked Jean-Philippe whether he could have a shower. He appeared in his underwear, his hair wet, and gave curt answers while he towelled his hair. No, not from London. Three months now. Serbian. But not really Serbian, Hungarian, it's complicated. Truth be told, Jean-Philippe wasn't really interested, they were pretty much the same thing to him.

The boy proved to be a gentle but confident lover, and didn't ask a single question about the flat for sale, or Jean-Philippe's past or present. After making love the boy lay limply on his front across the bed, and closed his bluish eyelids as though he hadn't been sleeping all afternoon.

Jean-Philippe ran his hand over his bum, along his shiny vertebrae and up to his neck. He brushed his hair aside to see the nape. The boy flinched as though he'd been touched in a sensitive area. All of a sudden he shifted onto his back and pressed his hair to the back of his head.

Jean-Philippe asked what was wrong. Whether it was sore. The boy kept an angry silence, staring at the ceiling. The older man was suddenly filled with some sort of dread. He thought, maybe this guy is sick, maybe he's got sores on him, or some other horrible thing. In fact, he doesn't even know who he is. He could be anyone. They didn't use a condom. In a dry tone, he asked him to get dressed and leave.

The boy didn't react, he carried on lying on his back motionless, and only rolled onto his front again when Jean-Philippe told him he'd call the police if he didn't get out of his flat within the next five minutes.

Again, the hand caressed from the bum, up his shiny vertebrae to the nape of his neck. He lifted the still damp, fair hair. The boy's nape was tattooed from left to right with different numbers.

'Were you in prison?' asked Jean-Philippe.

'No. Just. I had it done.'

'And what are the numbers?'

'Nothing. When I was born. Year, month, day, hour, minute.'

'Didn't it hurt?'

'So, being born hurts, doesn't it?'

Then he rolled over again. Jean-Philippe asked him one last time what the point was, and the boy answered, he likes it, end of. 'If I fall in battle,' he added in a foreign language, 'and someone is dragging me by my legs, then God will be able to read it.'

Two weeks later they stood in a plastic-panelled airport, where the boy was waiting for three other friends, so they could travel together to the Adriatic. Jean-Philippe filmed constantly, and was just recording tired families sitting idly on the benches. They'd been loafing about in this crumbling airport for five hours when the three friends finally ran in.

The friends arrived with a hired car and didn't light up in the car for Jean-Philippe's sake, but for the next two weeks the music blasted practically non-stop. At the first passport control, they handed over a French, a Hungarian, a Romanian, and two Serbian passports through the window, at which the customs person immediately asked them to step out because he'd like to inspect the inside of the vehicle. This would happen again a few times but the boys just laughed and chain-smoked their cigarettes as they leant against the car.

Jean-Philippe lifted the stained rucksacks thrust into his hands back into the boot with indifference, and he didn't make any attempt to understand the current relations, be they romantic relations or border relations. The Hungarian boy was seemingly with the Romanian, and during the second half of the trip Jean-Philippe ended up squeezed in beside the Romanian, since the Hungarian had moved into the driver's seat. The Romanian boy constantly wanted to light up a joint and had so many piercings on his face that

Jean-Philippe began to wonder whether he could kill him with an electromagnet. The four of them spoke Hungarian among themselves, and would toss him the odd English phrase now and again, out of which it was very seldom clear where they were going, why they were stopping and why they weren't going straight to the sea.

They were to go through Bosnia, but they wouldn't let the Romanian through without a visa, so in the north they crossed into Croatia. Looping around Bosnia and Herzegovina they drove towards the Croatian Adriatic, steadily becoming more dirty, more drunk and more penniless. In Split they stopped and bought themselves five identical black T-shirts with something written on them, which Jean-Philippe couldn't understand, but the rest found bloody hilarious. Later on they took the shirts off because there was no air-con in the car, and they travelled onwards, shouting, half-naked and covered in sweat. The piercing guy was right, nobody asked for their passports at the tiny border post hidden away by the Bosnian coast, then they drove the whole way along the Montenegrin coast drowned in dry sun. As a matter of form every day Jean-Philippe asked which country they were in, and then continued to drink the impossibly bad canned beer.

He'd never known the State Union of Serbia and Montenegro existed, but it undoubtedly did because after a certain point people suddenly wanted euros. By then the boys had spent all their Serbian dinars and Croatian kunas, so they stared at Jean-Philippe expectantly who had no other choice but to take out the rest of the money on his card. At the hotel the Serbian boy who travelled with a Hungarian passport slept with the Romanian, while the other Serbian, the blonde one, cut himself up and vomited all over himself. It was a difficult day. From here they intended to cut across Serbia back towards Vojvodina where Imi wanted to introduce Jean-Philippe—who had recorded an entire film's worth of interesting footage of jerking faces, yellow fields and abandoned houses—to some musician called Lajos, whom all four boys knew.

Jean-Philippe was dead tired. In the car, from one side he was being crushed by Imi, the Serbian or, rather, Hungarian boy, and from the other by the Romanian, you could barely even see out of the windscreen. Everyone was drunk, including the driver. A purple Slovenian lorry was driving in front of them, who knows where, and for minutes and minutes now they hadn't been able to over-take it. Singing, they swerved out into the road, then suddenly rolled, and continued their flight into the scorched fields of droning cicadas.

Jean-Philippe came around to a terrifying heavy silence and his first thought was that once again he'd survived something. From afar, he slowly began to hear the highway, the dashboard in front was nothing but blood. Everyone lay on their faces, except for the boy with the tattoo on the nape of his neck, who had fallen on the yellow grass, arms-spread, and on his back.

The Back's Story

The cricket didn't want to come out but it had scraped out the grass he'd poked in the hole, so he knew it was in there. The boy was lying on the ground in front of the hole and he was waiting to see what'd happen. He'd brought a cardboard box to keep it in for the way home. First he had to look good and close to see which one to take home, because he knew the only ones who made music were the ones with the yellow stripes on their legs.

The early summer sun was beating down hard, he'd burnt the nape of his neck and his shoulder-blades. There were a lot of ants on him too but he didn't crush them, he just slowly brushed them off so as not to scare the cricket. It was a long time before it came out: it had a look around, then climbed back inside. He carefully cut around the earth like a square of cake and lifted it into the box. The cricket must have been frightened of the big movement because it lay low and didn't make a sound, but now he knew for sure that it was in the cube of earth. He closed the box. He had to rush because the jackdaw was at home and he had to feed it too. He kept it outside in the shed so his brother's friends wouldn't tease him about it, or do anything to it.

He rushed home, he waded through the nettles down the hill so he'd reach the bottom row of houses where they lived quicker. In the village they called this bit the Flat, and the only people who lived on the Flat were the ones who had no money at all to move further in or move away. On the Flat there was no mains water, so people had to bring water from the common well. Since the families here hadn't paid their bills in years, the mayor decided he'd have that pump closed. Later a man from the city came out and told the families it was illegal, and that they have a right to water, but they just shrugged their shoulders. He was an outsider, at least they knew the mayor, even if everyone did hate him. But they didn't want to go into the council, they had enough problems already. They'd rather haul water in buckets from the well at the top of town—anyway, it wasn't an issue now, and hopefully it'd be solved somehow before the winter.

Last winter was a whole to-do as well, that's when people from the village came down because of them burning old rags—supposedly it was poisoning people up the hill. His parents really got mad that time, fine, they said, but the council should send us wood, because you can't so much as burn a twig from the village woods without getting reported by Bogdán.

All the families on the Flat bore grudges against Bogdán, and they guessed he might be to blame for putting forward the idea to the mayor's office of closing the pump. It had cost the mayor nothing, he stated on the radio that he had to keep the local residents' interests at heart, as though the bottom part of the village weren't residents. The boy didn't really understand this, but once with his little brother he'd thrown stones at Bogdán cycling past, then they'd hid in the long grass and watched as he examined his spokes and cursed. He saw him on his bicycle today, but today the boy was busy with the cricket.

He hoked out the fish tank from the shed and put the cube of earth inside. One of the sheets of glass was cracked right through, it wouldn't have done a fish but it was just right for a cricket. And he had to look for the jackdaw because it had hopped away, though he'd fenced it in.

He tossed aside all the dirty sheets of polycarbonate which his brother had carried back to put up on the roof later. The jackdaw was behind them. The dumb thing had keeled over because it was wrapped in surgical tape and couldn't balance properly, and now it lay there blinking at him from between two sheets.

He beat the rest of the soil out of the cardboard box and put the bird inside. He carefully undid the tape and checked how its wings were. They'd healed well but he had to bind them back up. He put a rag of cloth under the strip so it wouldn't stick to its feathers, then gave it some water with a syringe. His big brother was forever teasing him that he'd cook the jackdaw, but he answered back that you can't eat it anyway because they're poisonous. He knew his brother was only kidding but he still pushed the box into the back and walled it off with cardboard. He realized he was hungry too, so he headed off back into the village.

He went towards Bogdán's house, his cherries were ripe. He checked around to see if anyone was coming, but the old man lived alone and he'd seen him go past half an hour ago on his bike, so he knew he couldn't be home. Here, your narrator will happily add that while the boy had been fiddling with the tape, because one of the jackdaw's wing quills did get stuck to the surgical tape and he had to carefully free it, the old man had cycled back balancing a box tied on with bungees. Inside the cardboard box was a beaten-up old vacuum which he'd wheedled out of the Library. The Library in fact wasn't a library but an office of all sorts, and the vacuum hadn't worked for years but Bogdán said he'd get it going. He'd picked up the pipe the day before and leant it against the steps on the corner.

The boy clambered up and started eating the cherries. He stuffed a handful into his mouth then spat out the stones. That year there had hardly been any rain and the cherries hadn't split, they shone dark and ripe on the branches. He'd stained his mouth and his hands blue, he crammed as many into himself as he could reach.

After a while, he climbed a little higher and found a good branch where he could lean with his back against the tree and use both hands. Just when he was about to pull himself to a suppler branch, somebody asked from below, if the cherries were good. He was scared, it was Bogdán's voice. He looked down but he couldn't see anyone under the tree. The voice asked him again whether the cherries were good. That's when he saw that the old man was sat in the cellar entrance, looking in another direction. The boy was a bit confused by the friendly tone, so he answered, they are. 'Well, help yourself,' said Bogdán. The boy thought he'd rather climb down and run away but figured it'd be better to stay here a while first. 'Have as many as you like,' said the old man, 'I won't miss them.'

The boy crammed another handful into his mouth but didn't spit out the stones because, to his surprise, the old man had got to his feet and was making his way over to the tree. He stood there at the trunk and called up: 'If you come down, I'll give you something else. You can have a look around the house, I've all sorts here. Your brother and his pals were here too, they took anything they found, why shouldn't I let you do the same, no?'

The boy climbed down, but immediately something wasn't right and he wanted to get around the man standing directly in front of him. He got such a fright that he swallowed the rest of the cherry stones, as the old man drew the metal pipe from behind his back. The boy fell over and the old man started beating his back wherever he could. He was a bit worried for the vacuum pipe but he was so furious he wouldn't have minded if this little rat died right now before his eyes. At least it'd be one fewer. His brothers were always coming round, stealing anything they could lay their hands on, last time they'd even stolen his shit spade, now his old bicycle had gone. The Flat was crawling with these lice, they could rot in hell every one of them, and their mothers too.

He beat the boy for a long time, his strength was drained by the time he set the pipe down. The boy didn't move, so he brought water and poured it over him, and he told him, if he ever sees him or one of his brothers round here again, he'll kill them.

When the boy got back he didn't go into the small house but the shed and lay down on the cardboard. His brother found him when he got home with the wet clothes laid out under his back. The brother had brought home a bicycle but it was pure junk, he was going to take it apart for scrap.

He told his little brother him and his pals were going up to Budapest next week, everything's been arranged, they'll have somewhere to stay. If he can get a bit of money, he'll buy a hunter force combo and shoot the crap out of Bogdán. He'll bury him where no one'll find him. Or a power ranger night-vision mask, you can get one of them for a twenty, and he'll wait in the dark for the cunt up by the road. Holding a poultice to his back, the boy said he wanted to come up to Pest too with them, but then he wasn't sure because he remembered the jackdaw. He didn't dare ask what to do with it.

It wasn't until two weeks later he went up to his brother's, by then he'd been able to let the bird go. At first his brother helped him and tried to find him some work, in fact, he even lent him his phone once, because he had one now. But then he had a lot of work and all he said was, Take care of yourself, little man, and he disappeared for weeks. Now the brother was the one walking into the hospital. He couldn't understand at all what papers they were asking him for because it wasn't clear on the phone that his little brother had died.

They handed him a document which read:

The body is that of a slight-figured, dark-skinned young male of approx. 18–20 years. Irregular contusions all over the body, no signs of external injury to the

skull. Old secondary healed scars on both
arms. On the back are diagonally inverted
scars approx. 8–10 cm long, 1–2 cm wide,
presumably traces of an earlier beating.

He understood and he was in shock. His gaze
dropped to the bottom of the page, and he read
the very end of the long jargon:

In the lungs there is haemorrhaging of
both bronchi, and the mucus has a strong
odour, seemingly of solvents. Upon opening the skull, the brain is of average size.
Cause of death, bleeding in the abdominal
cavity, resulting in a two-stage rupture of
the spleen.

The boy asked whether all of this is connected
to his little brother, and where he was brought in
from. The pathologist replied that according to the
record somewhere in the Buda hills. The lad gave
a sigh of relief, whew, well it's not him then. It
can't be, sure, he'd never be all the way out there.
Let's go then, he said, now practically jolly, let's
see this lad you've mixed up with my brother.

CHAPTER TWENTY-SEVEN, OR

The Nose's Story

This one's difficult to write, what with there already being countless stories about the nose, famous ones among them too. Let's not write about the nose then, let's write about the pathetic fat man who serves as the wholesale store's warehouse security guard until seven in the evening when the guard with the dog arrives to relieve him.

He hadn't always been a security guard, previously he'd worked for two full years as a ticket inspector on Budapest public transport. Since he was a boy he'd always wanted to be a ticket inspector, but his mum had found him work in a relative's textile shop, so he could only apply after he turned thirty. He was mostly on duty on the 4 and 6 tram line, which was essentially one of the shittiest. Originally he'd wanted to request that he work buses, he'd always imagined himself walking up and down the bus, checking tickets, but life is no bed of roses, they said. Anyway, he still got an inspector's arm band. Back then he wasn't so fat; rather, he was prone to gaining weight, flat-footed and pudgy. He had a chin-strap beard and wore sunglasses, so he would look tougher. The identity card hanging round his neck could give some idea of how he looked at the time. The photo had been taken two years ago when he was taken on for the job, when he'd finished the course and passed the exam. In the picture he still had hair, but since then he'd shaved his head bald and gained thirty kilos. He is called Péter Kovaljov, there it is on the card.

So two and a half years ago Peti Kovaljov had had enough of being a ticket inspector, and applied for the body guard and security guard course. I'm afraid I can't refrain from adding that he was never fit to be a dog handler, since Peti Kovajlov was terrified of dogs. He could do daytime guard-ing of properties and that was his lot. He had to be home every night, his mum would lose her mind if he wasn't back by midnight. 'It's a danger-ous world,' she'd say, 'you just stay safe during the night!' But let's get back to dogs. And you can be sure his mum would gladly tell us why 'Petike' was so afraid of dogs. 'An Alsatian once jumped up on the poor thing on the pavement in front of his granny's house,' she'd rattle on. Let's not hear from her now, in case she bursts in on the story in hair rollers and slippers.

So when Peti was still a tram-ticket inspector, he'd be sweating down to his briefs if he ever had to step over some sprawled panting animal. He always required the faggots to display the extra ticket and to use a muzzle. He would never make it as a dog handler, but he didn't want to be a ticket inspector any more.

And he would have got used to everyone calling him an asshole, it's just that kind of work, it comes with the job. Getting called a dirty Jew and everything. He could take that. But that girl was the end of him.

He didn't like thinking back on it—we're only doing it out of necessity, so we have some means of pointing out the hidden connections.

Around Baross Street he regularly met a blond on his route. He avoided her, he never asked for her ticket. The girl just watched. He shrugged his shoulders, perhaps she didn't have a ticket. Every time he thought, next time he'll ask her, but then she wouldn't come for ages. When she popped up again, he'd be so happy that he wouldn't ask for it. He was sure she had no husband, she didn't seem the type who had. That's why he was so surprised when one time there was a little girl with her. When he approached them, he didn't ask for their tickets, he just looked down at the child. The little girl was clutching a blue plush elephant under her arm and stared up at him. He wanted to banter with her, and he asked her how old she was. He remembered that's what people asked children. The woman stared back at him and said, piss off, can't you see she's too young for a ticket? Dickhead. Then she got off the tram and repeated it once more from the pavement. She was in a black leather jacket, her blonde ponytail hung over the top of it, and once more, as if talking to the girl though everyone could hear on the tram: fat frigging pig. Like that. Fat frigging pig.

That's when Peti Kovajlov handed in his inspector's arm band. He applied for the new job on a pal's advice. It was a risky gig, they said, but he wasn't scared. He liked standing here with a firearm in the holster and he liked filling in the invoice when he was done. The best was the end when he left his John Hancock and tore it out— he got the money on the spot, cash in hand. He wasn't scared of robberies or burglaries. 'All they need is one look at me,' he'd say. 'If one of them comes closer, I stand my fucking ground and I tear them a new asshole.'

And nobody did go near him. By the afternoon there was nobody running the forklifts, the main gates wore closed, not a soul came anywhere near the warehouse entrance. The offices opposite were being renovated, the workers tossed out a few heating pipes and a bathtub, then they were off too. There's no way of telling whether there was some particular antecedent to the evening's events because from this point onwards, right from the early afternoon the whole affair is foggy.

What's certain is that that scrawny gypsy boy who turned up later behind the warehouse hadn't arrived yet. He was hanging about outside Tesco's, in case someone left some money in a shopping trolley. It was hot and he was cross, he considered going home but he would need money for the train. He'd come up to the city three months ago, of which he'd spent one with the metal scrappers and had enough of it. It was good for learning where everything was. Grub, the metal plant, those kinds of things. But you couldn't make any money at it. Then he tried begging for a while, using a crutch. No luck—twice he was mugged, and people gave him nothing. He couldn't find any gardening work, for that, they said, you'd have to go to the rich folk, over to Buda, but he didn't know his way around that side of town at all. True, once it had turned out he was in Buda because he'd rode too far on some bus, but that was pure chance. Here in the district at least he already knew a few places, that was better than nothing.

At around six in the evening the sun was still beating down hard, he thought his head was about to explode. He'd managed to pull together just enough change for one can of beer. He brought the beer round the back of the warehouse, that's when he saw the metal. He knew from scrapping where to give it in, so he went over to see what'd been thrown out. There was a bathtub, but he couldn't carry that, so he started sorting between the pipes. He felt the beer go to his head as he stooped over to work.

Opposite, from the far side of the road a big chunky guy was watching him, but he belonged to that warehouse, not this place. When he started separating the pipes the big guy came over and asked, what's going on. 'None of your business,' said the boy, and continued sorting because he'd spotted some scaffolding clamps at the bottom.

What came next is impossible to follow. All you could see was the fat one asked something again and the young one didn't look up. There's no telling whether he answered, but the chunky one suddenly stepped on his hand. At which point the young one tried to stand up and the guard stuck a boot firmly in his gut. The pain was so intense the boy pissed himself. The whole beer seeped out of him all warm. He stood up straight, hissing, 'The fuck you want, dickhead He lifted up one of the white pipes and started hitting him. The pipe was bent at the end and he used it to beat the bastard's flabby face. Dickhead, dickhead, dickhead. He pummelled his face and his nose until there was just a completely flat, bloody space between his eyes, as though there'd never even been a bump.

Péter Kovaljov fell into a deep sleep and ran down long bending corridors after the gypsy boy. Then he arrived at some large body of water, he had to cross it to keep up the chase. It was odd, his body didn't become lighter in the water but much heavier, he was barely moving forwards and his air had completely run out. He wanted to call out but only blood came out of his mouth. A mask was covering his mouth, and no one heard what he was trying to say. You could only have heard it from up close, but we could hear. Cocksucking fags—that's what he said. Of course, mistakes happen, there's no guarantee this is what he actually burbled.

They connected up the oxygen and he half came round. He could hear voices in the distance, strange sentences. Tube please, that's too small! An eight mil, are you blind? Inject a subclavian! Give him bicarbonate!

A sweating medical student was standing behind the doctor in the hospital corridor. He had to help with the CPR. He must have done something wrong, because Péter Kovaljov could hear irritated orders. He was up to his neck in water again, he was trying to walk, while the voices drifted over from the far shore: 'Press straight down, the bottom of the sternum! Come on. Not the middle! Stronger, there's no peripheral! Prepare the defibrillator!

Four minutes later the same medic was still standing on the corridor with a throbbing shoulder and a name in his hand. He was told to find the next of kin tonight and let them know.

The Knee's Story

The low afternoon sun shines bright through the large glass panes. The grey-haired and bony old man takes a last walk around the expansive studio. He's taking photos. He adjusts something, steps back and narrows his eyes.

He bends down, lies on his front and focuses. Behind him, in orderly rows lining the walls there are photos, all of them his own. But forget them. He's not just photographing details now but capturing the Whole.

He would like a picture from above. He starts to turn one of the metal cranks and the scaffold's wooden lift slides sideways. Dull creaking sounds echo around the big space. The structure is made of six crosspieces laid across vertical supports. A kneeling stool shifts left and right on each of the crosspieces. From these vantage points, any point of the Work is within arm's reach. The artist designed the structure himself a long time ago. At the time the Work was unrecognizable from its present state, but as it continued to build and grow he realized it would get more and more difficult to reach the top. Perhaps it would have been simpler to gather all the material first, and then put it together in its final form within a couple of weeks, but the gradual, imperceptible development was essential to the Work. He had always kept the image of the final outline in his mind's eye, waiting to be filled in with colour and a breath of life, so that one special day he could say, It's done.

While designing the scaffold, he kept thinking of Leonardo da Vinci, who built a lift-device while painting the Battle of Anghiari in order to work on the upper parts more easily. And every day it would cross the old man's mind that the Battle of Anghiari fresco was never completed. That the picture went to ruin because the master had got the ratios wrong when he was mixing the wax base.

Anything could have happened now too. Is that why over the many years he had felt he had to capture every single detail in a photo? So that at any time he could review and reconstruct the Whole? Not exactly. The details were necessary to continue, with the passing days every newly completed section forecast the work's completion.

He had begun kneeling towards the beginning. He didn't mean it as a form of penitence, it just happened. With time he discovered that the kneeling position was part of the artwork too, otherwise it couldn't have come to be. At first he bent, then sat, then squatted—he began with the outline. When he was tired of squatting, he knelt. From then on he would start in this position, changing the crushed pillows every two to three months, which—one after another—were flattened completely under his bony knees. He took a picture of each pillow before throwing it out, and a series of these photos lines the left-hand wall of the studio.

The series of photos on the opposite wall depicts his hand. Each picture shows it with another dried-out teabag, always in the same position. The teabag is pinched between forefinger and thumb, the thread barely visible. From a couple of meters away the hand looks like the detail of someone sitting in the lotus position. Jean-Philippe never comments on interpretations of his work. He offers the critic no reference points. He had got used to the kneeling position, and through the years his skin had hardened from the vajra-sana pose. For him kneeling was not about transforming greed into humility, it was just a practical position.

'Peace cannot be attained by those who strive to satisfy their desires, but solely by those undisturbed by their wishes' incessant flow, which floods into them like rivers into the ever filling, yet still ocean.'

Now and again the details faded and with time the colours changed. He had to be careful of that. And sometimes, though rarely, they darkened and had to be removed and stuck somewhere else. At first sight the Work looks like a shapeless mound. A heap of random bulges. But if we walk around it a few times, ever so slowly the shapes begin to take form. At least from a distance, from the far corner of the studio you can see that the mounds relate to one another. The Work is a man's body from the knee up, lying face down. His arms are cut off, or you could say they reach beyond the studio walls. He has no head either—the north wall slices it off at the neck like some sort of guillotine. His back is a sad, hulking slope of muscle. His buttocks are two neat, young hemispheres. The body is lying slightly askew, if he'd had legs, one would've certainly been drawn up. A sleeping Corpus between white walls.

The skin is brown. If we look closer, we can see every existing hue of the human skin. But the overall effect is something indefinable, a velvety dark. From a few feet away all you can see are pixels, dried-out teabags, but from further they blur into a single body.

Were the studio roof made of glass, we would see something else from above. But of course for that, for a full bird's-eye view, we would need to be much higher. Nevertheless, if there were an external eye, say if there was a God, who could see through walls like through people's skin, from up there the God would see the writing on the sleeping male torso. From the buttocks to the shoulders the darker teabags fuse into a barely legible phrase. Like some sort of bygone, fading tattoo. Written across the male body lying prone is Thirty Years.

The Birthmark's Story

The crowds are out at the park on the hill in the west of the city, there's barely a free parking space. Everything is covered in white powdery snow, it's as though they weren't in the same city they set out from half an hour ago. Back in their street the night's snow had already melted to grey slush, but the trees on the hill are lined top to bottom with frost, a packed bus is inching up the hill through thick snow.

The man and woman are making slow progress in the line of traffic, while on the lookout from behind the sweeping windscreen wipers for a space to finally free up. The little girl in the back is badgering them that they'll not have enough time, they'll have to go home soon, the sing-along CD ends for a second time.

Kids in anoraks and parents in sherpas clamber out of heated cars, get out a sled or clip on their skis and make for the slope. Our man slows down and indicates, finally they've found somewhere to park, a family in a Suzuki just left.

The space is narrow, the child can hardly get out on the left side, and the woman opens her own door carefully. A Renault Mégane is parked beside them, askew, as though it couldn't get in straight. Almost simultaneously with our newcomers, a thirty-something woman and a man get out of the back of the Renault. They go to the back of the car. They're a similar age as the majority of the day-tripping young parents around them. Our woman only needs to glance at them to know they'll lift a pram out of the car.

Two other, older people are sat in the front but they aren't getting out yet. The gaunt woman rests her hands on the wheel, on her finger is a surprisingly big angular ring. They're obviously the grandparents. But there's no child in sight—perhaps it's fallen asleep in the back and everyone's waiting. Our previous family meanwhile have left, tramping towards the field, leaning into the wind as it blows the snow in their faces. The man pulls up his hood, the mum stoops over the girl, looking for something. She turns back with the keys for the car and sees to her surprise that the man and woman parked beside them are opening up a black wheelchair with well-practised movements. The mum fetches the gloves out of the back of the car and watches them out of the corner of her eye.

The wheelchair is rolled to the front passenger's side. That's why they parked at such an angle, so they'd have space by the door. From the silhouette of the man sitting inside, you can see he's an older bald man, they lift him into the chair. The granny with the ring is standing ready with a red throw, and when the sick old man has been sat into the chair, she quickly spreads it across him and the younger man pulls a knitted hat on his head.

Our woman heads back, the dad is already meandering down the chopped-up piste with the shrieking girl. From above, from the tops of the leafless trees the enormous space is almost like a Bruegel, sprinkled with scampering characters, undiscernible from one another. Nobody, nobody on earth would guess that there was once something between the man in the wheelchair and our woman who went back for her daughter's ski gloves. Nor would they themselves think of it, after all, neither one of them recognized the other, and if fate doesn't will it, they won't cross paths on this snow-swept afternoon.

Seventeen years ago, yes, a long time ago, so long ago that the woman looked a bit more like the sledding girl than her current self, when the bus numbers in Budapest were different, and when the black pine of the future was but a sapling, well, seventeen years ago these two loved each other. The woman worked in an architectural practice called Industry Design as a freshly graduated architect. And the man as a building engineer, in the same place of course. The woman lived with her mum, who's been dead for years now, and the man lived with his wife and his three children, who've since grown up. We've actually seen two of them because the thirty-something man and woman aren't a married couple, they're the engineer's younger son and daughter. He has an older son as well, he hasn't appeared in this story, though at the time—as you know, when the black pine of the future was only a sapling—he played a crucial role in the then lovers' lives. He wasn't present then either, as he isn't now, but his nonpresence made him all the more important, since the lovers regularly met in his flat. At the time the woman was barely older than the boy who was studying in another town, and she used to curiously rifle through the humanities undergrad's book collection. As she was standing naked in front of the shelves, the engineer would always go up to her and lead her to the tall mirrored wardrobe. One by one he'd point at each of her birth marks. There were seven, one on her chin, three on her breasts, the rest were somewhere else. The rule of the game was that he'd list off all their names (Mole, Teeny, Weeny, Whosthat, Sneaky, Ugly, Frimple). The woman always insisted on this love game, even when they only had a quick hour. The couple in the mirror made her happy, and she'd tell the engineer that she could easily picture herself in this frame, but he'd bring up his children and that he was too old for a new family. He wasn't old, he was forty-nine, a man in his prime. He swam regularly, played tennis and fought bitterly against baldness. The woman always had to check whether the wicked little clearing on his crown had grown and she always said, Oh, not at all, it hasn't, but she could never put the engineer at ease, in going bald he felt haunted by inevitable ageing and death.

His wife—although the engineer was convinced she knew nothing—knew about the man's lover, just as she knew about the previous ones and all the ones to come. One thing, perhaps, she didn't know was that her husband was using their student son's flat for his trysts, that would possibly have been too much even for her, although she had already grown quite impassive by then. Later the engineer bought himself a little cottage in Villány in the south, though at the time they needed all their savings for their adult children. It's worth mentioning the double bed, exceptionally suited for love-making—not too hard, nor too soft—and the mirrored wardrobe, had both been bought by the wife, and she herself had seen to assembling them on that snowy day in the past when the black pine of the future was only a sapling, when the flat-packs of the once fashionable natural-finish furniture were delivered.

Husbands always think wives don't know about their lovers. The dad sledding with his daughter in his lap is absolutely positive that his wife suspects nothing, even though she (who was once a lover herself, as we've just heard) has known for months. When her husband goes away for a conference, it's enough to glance at the underwear and shirts in his suitcase to see he's not going alone or to a conference. She broods over it a lot, at Christmas she meant to bring it up as they were baking poppy-seed rolls. But right now she isn't thinking about it, for a change, instead she's thinking about getting a hot snack. She waves to the two distant figures and drawing in the air that she's going back to get some food.

At roughly the same time the daughter of the man in the wheelchair turns him on the path and pushes him in the direction of the strudel hut to get him some hot tea. The mum and youngest son are walking beside them, debating what sort of boiler to buy to replace the old one.

Our blond woman arrives at the small window, orders two slices of pizza, and is adding ketchup to one when she realizes she could get a strudel for her daughter as well, it's her favourite. She heads over to the neighbouring hut when the other group are just arriving. She's holding both slices in one hand. As she tries to take out some money with the other, she's rummaging about in her pocket when she bumps into the wheelchair by accident. A little ketchup plops onto the man's coat. 'Sorry,' she says, and glances down.

A couple of seconds pass as behind the yellow hollow-cheeked skull in the knitted hat she recognizes a former face. The eyes have changed the least. From below, the still amber eyes gaze up at her from the gaunt mask, as though to assure her that she's not mistaken. The man's brain, wasted by a tumour, suddenly aches as it leaps into action and, from the archives of the crumbling depths, thrusts the recorded names of the seven birth marks to the surface, as though he'd been asked to list off the seven seas, the Seven Chieftains of the Magyars or the seven dwarves. But the name of the woman he can't recall. Where the female name should be there throbs a painful scar, cut with a scalpel. 'Hi,' he says. His voice is truer to his former self than his body. 'Hi,' the woman answers, as though she hasn't noticed the state of him, as though it were possible to flick back and forth through the pages of time, to die, to rise again, to begin a story again and to break it all off again.

The wife behind the wheelchair hears them. It's already enough, she's heard all sorts of similar exchanges plenty of times before. Once for example, when the black pine of the future was only a sapling, she'd gone to the theatre with her husband. A woman arrived late, stopped at the end of the row and started making her way through to the middle. The wife just moved her knees to the side but her husband stood up. As the stranger in her lace dress passed them, she slightly brushed his suit with her dress and said, Hi. It was the same woman, with the birth mark on her chin—you couldn't not remember that.

The woman with the birth mark has got her poppy-seed strudel, and she sidles past them, as though she were again slipping between the theatre seats. She hurries in the wind towards the sledding slope and doesn't look back. The three people with the man in the wheelchair order all sorts, as the paper plates are passed to them one after the other through the hot window.

As they finish up, the young man wipes the icing sugar away from the old man's mouth, then his daughter bends over and gives him a handful of snow to clean his hands. But instead the old man rolls the snow into a ball, and with the kind of curiosity and desire, of which only children or those close to death are capable, he squeezes it.

CHAPTER THIRTY, OR

The Buttocks' Story

The woman with the pram is walking along Strada Universitatii, silently cursing the cars parked on the pavement. She turns onto Strada Avram Iancu, passes the university chapel, then Babeş-Bolyai University, and roughly by the end of this second sentence passes the entrance of Biasini Hotel. The previously mentioned buildings make no impression on her but the latter reminds her of a man she met a few years ago called David, who stayed a week in this hotel. She tilts the pram back, lowers it down the kerb and takes the direction of the cemetery. The toddler's head bobs as she naps and the woman's happy the bump didn't wake her up.

If we were to follow her movements from above, we would ascertain that her route exactly matches one made sixty-eight years ago on the same day and at the same time by a girl called Cosmina and her mother. It was sunny then too but Cosmina wasn't dozing, she was ambling along in her new laced shoes. But this woman is called Nazeli and she knows nothing of that. What a curious thought—the fabric of our lives. The human body pops up and submerges in time, then surfaces again in memory, up and down, up and down, like a needle, seaming together the fraying layers of the past and the present. Everything is sewn together while the thread itself is invisible.

The toddler in the pram does come around and starts to whine because she's thirsty. The woman searches through the basket underneath for the drink and the trainer lid for the top. She bends over, hushes the child and stuffs the plastic bag back in the basket to cover her purse.

If she was to look behind her, she'd notice the man in the blue shirt who's been staring in raptures at all this bending over. He stepped out of the Biasini Hotel and, no exaggeration, he followed the woman's bum the whole way. Even after childbirth this bum has stayed shapely and round, set off nicely by the close-fitting cotton skirt.

He has a camera and tripod and he was heading to the cemetery to take some shots of the place. He's been doing the same for days now but today's light is particularly nice. He walks behind the woman and is happy to see they're going to the same place. In the cemetery he loses sight of her for a while but resolves to take a couple of shots of her later. The woman is stunningly youthful and would look good in the colour photo essay he's putting together for the foreign magazine's spring issue. He can imagine some catchy title for it, like Youth and Motherhood, or Life in Death's Garden. He's sure the woman wouldn't say no, but first he has to finish yesterday's series on famous graves while the sun is still shining so brightly.

The long-haired brunette has gone in the opposite direction. The photographer doesn't see that the little girl has climbed out of the pram and is running about. Later she hunkers down at the base of the resting place of Dr András Nagy, Calvinist theology professor, and tries to pee in the grass. It's a novelty for her not wearing a nappy, she enjoys the freshly acquired skill, and of course the liberated botty. Alas, she's still unable to take care not to pee all over herself, so her mother quickly grabs her and lifts her up from behind. The girl gets angry at this and doesn't need to go any more. A little later, behind the gravestone of Mrs József Sebestyén née Rozália Pauler she tries again, successfully, getting pee on both her shoes. The photographer has lost sight of them, which isn't a bad thing, because any kind of inappropriate look would've annoyed the woman. The magazine reporter doesn't know yet, but we do, that he'll never get that picture. The toddler climbs back into the pram and trundling along they stroll around the cemetery. The photographer is just looking for the right angle on some Turkish-sounding man's grave when he sees the woman pass by. They aren't heading towards the exit, they're going towards the inside fence of the cemetery. Broken chicken wire separates this part of the graveyard from the old Jewish cemetery on the Strada Republici side. The woman goes towards the section where the wire is almost completely trampled. She lifts the pram over, and then the girl. They like strolling in here because there's never anyone around.

As she's fiddling with the pram her phone rings but she can't pick it up. The man who's calling is sitting in the senior consultant's office of a Bucharest hospital. He meant to call much earlier but first the head nurse came in, then he had to handle an official call. The call had lasted a fair bit of time and had visibly irritated David, who eventually raised his voice saying, Măta-n cur,* at which the head nurse, who had just returned with

* Fuck your mother's ass.

a photocopy, commented in appreciation how excellently the doctor's Romanian was coming on.

The hands of the long-haired woman are now free, so she calls the number back, and in Bucharest the head nurse leaves the office again. The girl is wandering about among the graves, her mum keeps one eye on her at all times. The woman paces up and down, distractedly pulling at weeds, then finds a grave completely covered in moss, half sunk into the earth, and sits on it. She smooths the cotton skirt under her bum and carries on speaking. The child likes the idea of talking on the phone and sits beside her. She holds her biscuit to her ear and makes a call herself. If someone were to clear away the moss under the woman's chilling bum, and to scrape out the completely illegible, dirt-filled engraving, they'd see the name of the deceased was Áron Kozma. But nobody has visited the grave for years, so the engraving remains illegible for ever. The toddler meanwhile has eaten her telephone. The woman hangs up and leans back on the stone a little, so that between the boughs of the trees her face might catch the spring sun.